THE CHILD OF CALAMITY SERIES
OMNIBUS EDITION

LISSETTE E. MANNING

L.D.B. Press

Power Play
The Child Of Calamity Series
Omnibus Edition
Books 1–3

To those I hold near and dear to my heart.

This one's for you!

TABLE OF CONTENTS

TABLE OF CONTENTS

TABLE OF CONTENTS

TABLE OF CONTENTS

ACKNOWLEDGMENTS

There are so many to name that the list is endless. Instead, I'll acknowledge all of you in one fell swoop.

Thanks so much to each and every one of you who's always believed in me. Your never-ending support goes a long way. I am forever grateful for all the insights and feedback, the lovely messages, and the love you've shown me. Thanks for always inspiring me!

To my family and friends, thank you for always being there when I need you. I love each and every one of you!

To my readers and fans, you mean a lot to me. You are the ones who continuously move me to jot down the craziness that goes on inside my head. I honestly hope you enjoy these stories I write. There's more to come, I assure you.

To The-One-Who-Shall-Not-Be-Named, you are never far my thoughts and heart. Never does a day go by when I don't think of you. It's awesome to see how far you've come, Sweetheart. I'm proud of you!

AUTHOR'S NOTE:

Fair warning, Lovelies.

I've taken a little literary license with the Greek gods and goddesses. I thought I should mention this, because several relationships throughout the series itself are not cannon. Some find themselves in situations they normally wouldn't, and I've tweaked their usual details to suit the purpose of the stories/serics itself.

For example, while Artemis might be known as one of the chaste virgin goddesses, she's anything but chaste. She does things to suit her purposes, and has a voracious appetite/attitude to match. She has an agenda to fulfill, and will do everything possible to make sure things are done to her specifications.

I apologize in advance for the literary license I've taken with the characters and their purported histories. I do hope none of you mind me doing so. After all, anything is possible when writing fiction, right?

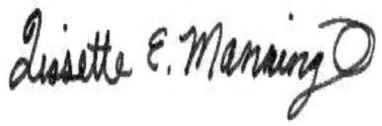

THE CHILD OF CALAMITY SERIES
BOOK 1

The
Goddess's
Wishes

LISSETTE E. MANNING

Her wish is their command.

Artemis has a plan. Her eye has fallen on the throne of Olympus, and she'll do anything to get it. She knows Zeus won't give it up so easily, but she's determined to dethrone him, none-the-less. Her father is known for his infamous romps amongst the mortals. Surely, there must be something she can use against him?

When her attention is drawn to Callidora Spiros, she soon realizes that her father does indeed have secrets. Brazen and beautiful, the girl piques her interest in more ways than one, though Artemis isn't quite sure as to how she's truly tied to the gods. Intent on discovering what her father has kept hidden for so long, she'll need as much help as she can get.

Demanding and willful, Artemis has been known to achieve her every whim. With the bat of an eyelash, or a simple word, she's wrapped many a man around her little finger. The gods, on the other hand, aren't so easy to bring around. Never-the-less, she's going to do everything possible to gain the upper hand. Mount Olympus will be hers, with or without the help of the other gods and goddesses.

CHAPTER 1

Artemis materialized in the middle of her brother, Apollo's, bedroom with a resounding pop. A smile of satisfaction spread across her lips as she watched him scramble out of bed in search of his clothes. A look of annoyance clouded the features of the demigoddess lying on his bed, clutching the bed sheets tightly to her chest.

Her silvery-yellow eyes narrowed as she stared at the demigoddess, Dyina, and pointed to the adjacent door. "Get out!"

"Damn it, Artemis!" Apollo growled as he tugged his chiton into place. "Can't you knock?"

Artemis grinned, and made her way toward the chaise lounge tucked into the left corner of the room. "Where's the fun in that, brother?" she quipped, lowering her slender frame onto the settee.

The demigoddess rummaged about the room for her clothes, her blue eyes sending imaginary vicious daggers in Artemis' direction. The goddess's smile never faltered as she watched her brother and his current paramour move about Apollo's chambers. He took a moment to show Dyina to the door, his shoulders taut with tension as he swung the door closed.

"I'm assuming you're here for a favor of some kind?" Apollo asked, running a hand through his thick blond curls.

"Something like that."

He approached the table nearby, and poured himself a glass of red wine. He knocked back his drink in one gulp, and promptly poured himself another before taking a seat on the chair in front of the lounge upon which she reclined.

"What now?"

She bestowed him with a knowing gaze, her lips quivering with effort as she tried to hold back her excitement. "I want Mount Olympus, brother, and you're going to help me get it."

He snorted with amusement, and downed the glass of wine. "A lofty goal, Sis, but that's not likely."

Her smile disappeared, her eyes narrowing to half slits. "I expected more from you."

He summoned the pitcher of wine, and filled his glass once more. "Do you honestly think dear old Dad is going to give up the throne so easily?"

"No, but that's where you come in. He owes us. Besides, we've always been his favorites."

"Whether he owes us or not, Artemis, you'll never get him to step down."

"Not yet, but I will. And when I do, Mount Olympus

will be mine!"

Apollo tossed his head back, and laughed heartily. "There's a good many of us with an eye on Daddy's throne. You're not likely to get it, nor are any of us."

Her nostrils flared outward with anger as she stared at her twin brother. "You owe me."

"I'll pay up. Eventually."

She sat up straight, staring deep into her brother's eyes. "You'll pay up now, brother dear. Zeus has been careless, and I intend to unmask him before the other gods and goddesses."

"How, pray tell?"

A photograph materialized in thin air as she flicked her hand about. He deftly caught the glossy paper between his fingers, and examined it.

"Who is she?"

"I suspect she's one of Daddy's illegitimate children. The one the prophecy speaks of."

His lips pursed with concentration. "Prophecy?"

She nodded. "Yes. The *Child of Calamity*, Apollo. She's the one. I feel it."

Apollo wracked his brains as he did his best to remember the prophecy she spoke of. Unfortunately, nothing came to mind.

"She doesn't look like anything special. The girl looks like she's completely mortal."

"Appearances can be deceiving."

"Yes, and she seems harmless enough. How old is she anyway?"

"She's nineteen, and she lives in New York."

"New York? Really?"

"Yes. Her mother's certainly striking, so I can sort of understand what Zeus sees in her."

His brow furrowed as he examined the photograph once more. "What does this have to do with me?"

She smiled, her eyes shining with delight. "You're going to fetch her for me."

"Me?" he sputtered with disbelief.

"Yes. You're the perfect candidate, Apollo," she breathed as she shifted her position, and leaned closer to him. Her lips hovered above his own. "You're hard to resist."

The picture fluttered to the floor as Apollo's stormy blue gaze fell upon her mouth. "If that is so, then why do you resist me on occasion?"

She frowned, and pulled herself out of his reach. "You're my brother!" she mumbled as she pushed herself to her feet, and strode toward the open window.

He followed her, and wrapped his arms around her. Apollo brushed his lips along the curve of her neck, playfully nipping at her flesh. "That's never stopped you before."

"Damn it, Apollo!" she grated, and disengaged herself from his embrace. "Not now. We've other matters to attend to."

He snorted with derision. "Attend away!"

Her heart hammered within her chest as she stared at him. She wanted very much to give in to what she was feeling, but she knew she couldn't. Not now, anyway. If she was to succeed in having her plans fall through, she needed to be strong. Falling prey to her baser desires right now would not bode well.

Squaring her shoulders, she replied, "You need to find her, and bring her to me."

Apollo's mouth thinned to a tight line. "You could make that happen with a flick of your hand, Artemis. I honestly don't see why you need me to do your dirty work."

"You are the *God of Light*, brother, and the sun itself. With your position high above the world, you see and hear everything. The only one who has a better chance in finding her than any of us combined is you."

"For someone who's known as the chaste huntress, you sure as hell don't make use of that damned title! You're supposed to be a protector, of sorts, too. Yet here you are entreating me to hunt a woman you deem to be the *Child of Calamity*. That's a massive contradiction, don't you think?"

She crossed her arms about her chest, her chin rising with determination. "If you won't help me, Apollo, then I'll get someone else to do it."

"I never said I didn't want to."

"Yeah? Well, you sure as hell are acting like you are. Think of the power we could garner by working together. If we take out the one thing he loves the most, then Daddy dearest won't know what hit him. This woman is the one the prophecy speaks of. I'm sure of it. Why else would she be so well protected?"

Apollo frowned. "How come I've never seen this young woman until now?"

"You never pay attention to things unless it's really necessary. You obviously prefer your trivial pursuits over the needs of the court, thus you've no true knowledge of what goes on here on Mount Olympus."

"That's not true!" he balked.

"Yes, it is!"

Displeasure flickered across his face. "You know what? Get someone else to do your dirty work!" he replied haughtily, and orbed himself out of the room.

Artemis stared at the spot he'd been standing in, moments ago, with dismay. She'd wanted her brother's help in more ways than one. Deep inside, she'd assumed he'd be easy to bring over to her side. Unfortunately, she'd been mistaken on that account. An idea soon popped into her head as she stood there pondering her current predicament. She smiled, her eyes gleaming with ruthless cunning.

No matter, she thought. *I've other ways to make things happen.*

She glanced about her brother's room one last time before she dematerialized, intent on putting her plans into motion, one way or another.

CHAPTER 2

"Is there a reason you've decided to set foot into my realm, Artemis? It better be important!" Hades barked as he tossed a stack of papers across his desk.

She smiled broadly as she popped up near a dais her uncle had placed in front of the fireplace. "It is," she assured, tossing her auburn hair over her left shoulder.

He quirked an eyebrow in her direction, and crossed his arms about his chest. "Oh?"

She pursed her lips, running her fingers across the dais's soft fabric. "I need you to help me find someone."

Hades' eyes narrowed with suspicion. "For?"

Artemis' heart thumped rapidly within her chest as she realized she'd come to the wrong person for help. "A long-lost family member."

He laughed heartily, and shook his head. "Did you honestly think I'd fall for that?" he quipped, and dropped his six-foot-two frame onto his chair. "I'm familiar with each and every member of our family, Artemis. Some

7

quite personally, so whatever claims you were going to make are invalid."

"You don't know about this one. Nobody does. I came across her by accident. Daddy dearest has kept her well hidden."

"You've been trailing one of Zeus' offspring?"

"Yes. I doubt you've an idea as to whom I speak of, though."

"You have proof?"

"Of?"

"That she was sired by Zeus."

"Some."

He settled back against his chair, and produced a pitcher of wine in front of him. The decanter floated gently onto the desk. A goblet appeared in the air, fluttering toward him. He caught the cup in mid-air, and poured himself a glass, waiting for her to continue.

"I'm waiting."

"For what?"

"Proof."

She presented him with a perfect pout. "You won't take my word for it, Uncle?"

He knocked back his drink in one gulp, and shook his head. "No. I know you, Artemis. Your hunting comes with unwanted benefits. I'm not sure as to what you want this person for, but it can't be good."

"She's piqued my curiosity, that's all."

"I beg to differ."

She growled with frustration, and snapped her fingers together. The photograph she'd shown Apollo not too long ago floated in his direction. He plucked the piece of paper out of the thin air, and scanned the picture. A muscle jumped across his jaw as he gazed upon the young woman's face.

"Where did you get this?"

She shrugged nonchalantly. "Deivos brought it to me."

"How did he come across this?"

"I'm not sure."

His nostrils flared outward with anger. "Yes, you do."

She shook her head with vehemence. "No, I don't. He wouldn't tell me. I've tried everything I could think of to try to make him talk. Trust me on that."

Hades smirked with amusement. "I'm surprised your feminine wiles didn't work to your advantage."

"He's a demigod, Uncle. Not all demigods fall under my spell," she replied haughtily.

"Where is he now?"

"New York, I gather."

"Bring him to me."

An appalled expression spread across her face. "I'll do no such thing!"

He tossed the photograph aside. "Then expect no help from me."

"But . . ."

"None, Artemis. Have I made myself clear?"

She clenched her teeth together to keep herself from verbally lashing out at him. "Yes, Uncle."

He nodded, and flicked his hand at her in dismissal.

"You may go."

She sighed softly as she kept her eyes pinned on him. Without another word, she orbed herself out of Tartarus. She'd lost yet another consort, but she wasn't out for the count. At least, not yet. There were a good many whose services she could employ to do her bidding. She just needed to find the right person for the job. With a knowing smile playing about her lips, she sped off to Mount Olympus, hopeful that she'd find someone to follow through on her requests soon enough.

CHAPTER 3

A startled cry was rent from Artemis' lips as she strode into her room. Her half-brother, Hermes, lay across her bed, his shrewd gaze centered on her face. She gathered her composure, and held her head high as she walked further into her chambers.

"What are you doing here?" she asked as she made her way over to the washing basin.

Hermes examined his fingernails, a knowing smile upon his lips. "Our dear brother mentioned that you might need me."

Her eyes narrowed with suspicion as she glanced at him over her right shoulder. "Oh?"

"Apollo wasn't wrong, was he?"

She turned away from him, and grabbed a small scrap of cloth resting next to the basin. She dipped it in the lukewarm water, and wrung the excess water out. Normally, she left such trivial tasks to her servants, but she wasn't in the mood to deal with their attentions. Her servants meant well, but sometimes, she found their presence a tad annoying. Most especially when they fawned over her repeatedly.

"What did he tell you?" she asked as she ran the cloth across her collarbone.

"Not much, actually. Just that you required my assistance."

She rolled her eyes. "Why would he think that?"

He shrugged, and pushed himself off of the bed. "You tell me."

She drew the cloth across the expanse of her shoulders, uncaring about the fact that the peplos she wore was getting wet. Hermes approached, and pulled the washcloth out of her grasp, dropping it into the basin. He turned her around, and clasped her chin between a thumb and forefinger, gently pulling her head up.

"What's going on, Artemis?"

She bit her lip, wondering as to whether she could trust him. Though he'd done her bidding many times in the past, there was no telling how he'd take the news that she was plotting to overtake the throne. He and Zeus got along well, and she was well aware of just how tight his relationship with her father was. Should she take one wrong step, he was likely to betray her at a moment's notice.

She pulled her chin free of his hold, and offered him a smile. "Nothing, brother. Apollo and I had a disagreement, that's all."

"About?"

"This and that," she replied airily.

He frowned. "Are you sure?"

She nodded. "Yes."

Hermes unclasped the pouch strapped to his waist, and dug within its depths. He found what he was looking for, and held a piece of paper aloft in her direction. Her heart pounded inside of her chest as she stared at his offering.

"What's that?"

"Take it."

She was hesitant to do so. "Why?"

He stormed toward her, and dropped the paper into her hands. She looked down, and realized that the parchment wasn't just a piece of paper. The very photograph she'd shared with Apollo and Hades lay in her hands. How her brother had gotten a hold of a copy of it, she did not know. Yet the fact that he had spoke volumes. He might have been angry with her, but he was still willing to assist her with her plans. That thought alone pleased her.

"Who is she?"

"I'm not sure, but I'm of the mind to find out."

"Apollo mentioned something about the prophecy concerning the *Child of Calamity*."

On guard, she rose to her full height of five-feet-eight. "What exactly did he say?"

"Not much, actually. He asked me about the prophecy. I tried to explain things to him, but he seemed way too distracted. It was almost time for the sun to crest over the Earth to signal a new day, so he wasn't that forthcoming about what he wanted. He had time enough to hint that you needed help, however."

Her taut stance relaxed. She made her way to the nearest table, scrumptious food spread across its entire surface. Plucking several green grapes off of a plate, she tossed the succulent orbs into her mouth.

"I see."

"Are you going to tell me what you're up to?"

She glanced in his direction as she poured herself a cup of wine. "What I need, dear brother, requires complete secrecy. Not even Zeus must know."

His mouth thinned to a tight line. "You're not planning to incite Father's wrath, are you?"

She feigned a look of abject horror. "God, no!" she gasped, and ate three more grapes.

The expression on Hermes' face told her that he did not quite believe her. "You are, aren't you?"

"Do I look as if I'd do such a thing?"

He wrapped his arms around his chest, staring down at her with displeasure. "You have in the past," he pointed out.

"That was then, Hermes. I was young and carefree. The world was my oyster back then. I admit that I did things I'm not proud of, but I've changed. Besides, Daddy dearest has forgiven me for my past indiscretions."

He rolled his eyes at her, not quite taking her words at face value. "You might seem so innocent and demure, Sister, but we all know you're not. You're up to something."

She nonchalantly waved a hand through the air in

hopes of shrugging off the sense of unease that threatened to overcome her. She was strong and independent. Willful, at times, too. Yet she'd never cowered before anyone aside from her father. If she was to succeed in accomplishing her current goals, she needed to remember that.

"I'm not," she lied, her tone deceptively sweet. "I'm just curious as to who this woman is. She's tied to us somehow, Hermes. I need to be sure that she's not a threat to our existence."

He dropped his tall frame onto the nearest chair, his lips pursed. "You honestly believe she's family?"

"Yes. Why else would she be so well guarded?"

He shrugged. "She's human, Artemis. There's a good many reasons as to why her caretakers protect her so thoroughly. Perhaps you're putting too much into things? There's a possibility she's not even what you think she is," he reasoned.

Her jaw tightened with frustration. "I'm never wrong, brother."

"That's debatable."

"What does that mean?"

"Your passion has clouded your judgment on occasion. Yes, you're strong and decisive. You're able to maintain your calm whenever possible, but you often lose yourself to the emotions running through you, allowing yourself to falter when you should not. This is one of those times. This woman seems harmless. She's nothing you should worry about."

Anger burned in the depths of her eyes. Hermes was

right, but she would not admit it to him. She would not allow him to point out more of her flaws at whim. Nor would she buckle beneath the onslaught of his words. She realized, then, that his assistance was one she could do without. Though he was a formidable adversary, his allegiance to their father was apparent. Should she take one wrong step, he'd thwart her plans in an instant.

A cold mask settled upon her face as she calmly replied, "You know what, you're right."

"I am?"

She nodded. "Yes. I shouldn't soil my hands with such trivial matters. I'm obviously mistaken. You said it yourself; she's nothing but a human. Mortals are beneath us, right?"

He sat up straight, a guarded expression on his face. "Yes, they are," he agreed. "This insignificant creature doesn't deserve our attention. You should set your sights on something more important."

"Like what?"

He grinned, his blue eyes shining with mischief. He spread his arms wide. "We're on Mount Olympus. Food, drink, and countless days of debauchery are our lofty goals. Set aside your worries, Sister. Enjoy the life you've at your fingertips!"

A corner of her mouth lifted with amusement. "I shall!" she said, turning her attention back to the food sitting on the table. "Now, if you don't mind, get out."

His smile faltered. "You're serious?"

She looked at him out of the corner of her eye, tossing a piece of cold venison into her mouth. "Yes. Get out."

His mouth tightened, and his nostrils flared with anger. Without another word, he disappeared, leaving her to her own devices.

Artemis sighed with relief, and dropped onto the chair behind her. She listlessly picked at the plate of food in front of her, her mind reeling with the implications of what she and her half-brother had discussed. Hermes wouldn't keep quiet for long. He'd find a way to gather more information about the girl in the photograph soon enough. She was sure of it.

She needed to keep him from doing so, and soon. He'd ruin her carefully constructed plans otherwise. The question was, how could she do so without soiling her hands further in the process?

CHAPTER 4

"A penny for your thoughts?" Poseidon inquired as he sat down on the bench next to Artemis.

She looked up with surprise. "Uncle!"

He chuckled softly, his blue-green eyes roving across the expanse of the immaculately kept garden spreading out before them. "You rarely venture out this way, my dearest niece. Is something wrong?"

She nibbled on her lower lip in thought, basking in the peace and quiet the garden offered those who tread within its depths. "No," she said a tad too quickly.

"Artemis . . ."

She looked down, picking at the folds of her peplos's skirt with the edge of her fingernails. "It's just the usual. I worry about those under my care. The animals and the young women I present myself to. People seem distracted these days, and barely offer us thanks for the blessings we bestow upon them."

He regarded her through veiled eyes. "Are you sure

that's it?"

She nodded absently. "Yes."

"Why do I think otherwise?"

She'd forgotten how perceptive her uncle truly was. At seven-feet-six inches tall, he exuded an aura of strength and masculinity that rivaled no other. He used his charm and swarthy good looks to his advantage. Women, and men, fell at his feet whenever they lay eyes on him. She often wondered if he enjoyed such attention, or whether he got bored of being revered quite so often.

"It's nothing."

He reached out to clasp her hand, patting it gently. "You can trust me."

She kept her eyes focused on the lush green grass below her feet. "Can I?"

"Have I ever failed you?"

"No."

"But?"

She looked up at him, and frowned. "Hmmm?"

"There's an unspoken *but* hovering in the air."

A soft chuckle slid past her lips. She'd forgotten how easily her uncle could pull her out of her sulking moods. "Sort of."

"So . . ."

Artemis gazed into the depths of her uncle's eyes, wondering if she could truly trust him. Her consorts in finding the *Child of Calamity* had failed her, thus far, and part of her was afraid to seek out the help of one of the higher gods or goddesses. Common sense told her that it wouldn't hurt to ask him for his opinion on the matter.

Though she ran the risk of losing everything she'd strived for in the process, something she refused to allow.

"I've been looking for someone," she said, moments later.

"Anyone I know?"

"I'm not sure."

"Is this person here on Mount Olympus?"

"No."

His eyes focused on her slumped form. "Who?"

"A mortal."

"A mortal?"

"Yes. A woman, to be exact."

He sat back against the bench, and crossed his arms upon his chest. "You've never been one to be so fixated on lesser beings. What's changed?"

She turned to face him, her eyes narrowed slightly. "Can I trust you?"

"Artemis . . ."

"If I'm to tell you what I know, I have to be sure that you won't throw me to the wolves."

His jaw clenched tight. "I wouldn't."

"Yes, you would. You've betrayed people in the past, Uncle. Mostly when it suits you in order to gain the upper hand, but still . . ."

He sighed, and pinched the bridge of his nose between a thumb and forefinger. "I've done things I'm not proud of. I admit it, but when it comes to those I love, I do my best to protect them. Except Zeus. He can rot in Tartarus for all I care."

She laughed, and shook her head. Unbidden, tears

pricked her eyes. "And you'd protect me?"

"If it came to that."

Her mouth trembled as she fought to retain her composure. "I want to believe that."

His heart constricted as he noticed the bright sheen of moisture shining in her eyes. "You should. Now, tell me about this woman. Why does she vex you so?"

"She doesn't vex me. Not exactly. It's what she represents that draws me to her."

"And?"

She bit her lip once more. "I believe she's the *Child of Calamity*."

His eyes opened wide. "The *Harbinger of Chaos and Destruction*?"

"Yes."

"How did you come by this knowledge? What does she look like?"

Her heart hammered within her chest as she saw the calculating glint in his eyes. "I . . . My source is irrelevant."

"Unless you tell me exactly what I need to know, I can't help you, Artemis."

"If I'm to divulge said information, I require a favor in return."

Poseidon stood up, looking down at his niece in contemplation. She was up to something. He sensed it. Whenever something or someone caught her attention, it led to consequences that were usually out of her control. She had a knack for both getting into trouble and inciting it. Artemis might look sweet and virginal, but she was nothing like what she portrayed herself to be. She was cold, cunning, and quick to the cut.

"And what favor would that be?"

Artemis pushed herself to her feet, gliding toward the stone wall nearby. She pressed her hands against it, her mind working hard to come up with a plan that would benefit her in the long run. Poseidon would make a formidable consort, she realized. He detested Zeus' ruling far more than any of the other gods and goddesses. If she were to bring him completely to her side, she'd be able to use his talents to her advantage whenever possible. Though, she needed to be careful to not divulge more than what was necessary in order to keep her uncle from knowing about her exact plans for Mount Olympus.

"I'll get back to you on that."

"You do that. I'll be waiting to hear from you soon. Whatever you're up to, Artemis, it does not bode well. Be careful with what you do. You wouldn't want to make enemies of those who are willing to support you."

With that, he disappeared. Her heart raced as she stared at the horizon. Poseidon was aware of the fact that she wasn't being truthful with him. He would not remain passive with the situation at hand. He, too, would search for the *Child of Calamity*. She could not allow him to find her. She would make it possible for Artemis to bring her father to his knees. The throne would be hers, one way or another. No one would take it from her.

CHAPTER 5

Artemis' mind wandered as she walked down the halls of her home on Mount Olympus. Servants hurried about preparing a feast in honor of her return, as well as making sure that everything was spic-and-span. Her handmaidens trudged at her heels, eager to catch her up on the goings-on inside the home. While she was grateful for their company, and enjoyed their exuberance immensely, she found their presence a tad cumbersome at that given moment.

She dismissed them, and continued on to her bedroom, intent on taking a warm, calming bath. Pushing the door closed behind her, she strode toward the bathroom, pulling off her clothes as she moved along. A smile of delight crossed her face as she eyed the large tub of hot, steaming water standing before her.

She added several drops of rose oil to the water, mixed it in with a flick of her hand, and stepped into the tub. A sigh of pleasure and relief slid past her lips as she leaned back, and comfortably settled into the water. She kept her eyes closed, and allowed her hands to roam across her breasts.

A frisson of awareness rippled through her as she pinched her nipples between her thumbs and forefingers. Her breath grew ragged as her body came to life. Artemis slid her right hand downward, and lightly trailed her fingertips across her navel toward her aching mound. She slipped a finger past her pink folds, rubbing her clit ever so gently.

She spread her legs wide, allowing the water's heat to amplify the warmth gathering at the tender juncture of her thighs. With a quick flick of her hand, her fingers slipped inside, her muscles clenching tight around the slick digits. She worked the appendages back and forth, and moaned aloud as she allowed herself to climax.

Basking in the afterglow of her orgasm, she was not aware of the unexpected presence inhabiting her bathroom. Her eyes flew open with surprise as the water began to bubble around her, coaxing another orgasm from her depths. Apollo stood before her in all of his naked splendor. Her heart hammered within her chest as she stared up at him.

"What are you doing here?" she asked as he stepped into the tub.

A knowing smile played about his lips as he saw her clamp her legs together. He rubbed his aching cock, keeping his eyes on hers.

"I wish to pleasure you," he said, reaching out to wrap his hands around her knees.

She cursed the tub's limited mobility as he shoved her thighs apart, intent on sliding between them. In the blink of an eye, she found herself wrapped in a towel on the other side of her room. Apollo glared at her, upset by the fact that she'd thwarted his attempt in gaining satisfaction.

"That's not necessary," she said, as she clutched the towel tightly to her.

"You mean to leave me unsatisfied?"

"You have a multitude of chits at your disposal. Surely, you do not need me?"

He stood up, and stepped out of the bathing tub, water coursing down his muscular body as he moved toward her. "They are not you, Artemis. None know how to pleasure me the way you do."

Her eyes closed of their own volition as he reached out, and curled a hand around her cheek. Artemis' body ached for fulfillment, but she knew it had to be denied. With a quick jerk of her head, she pulled herself out of his grasp, and strode toward the wardrobe where all of her clothes were kept. She selected a dress made of the finest silk, and allowed the towel to drop to the floor.

She tugged the fabric over her head, and carefully pulled it into place. Next, she drew forth a pair of dainty red slippers, and slipped her feet into them. Artemis approached her vanity table, and sat down. She picked up her hair brush, and ran it through her auburn tresses. All the while, she tried to ignore her brother's imposing presence.

Apollo snapped his fingers together, and manifested

a white chiton with a yellow sash upon his tall frame. Brown leather sandals encompassed his large feet. He made his way over to her, and settled his hands upon her shoulders. Their gazes clashed as they stared at one another through the vanity's mirror.

"Deny it all you want, Sister," he breathed, "but your body craves for what I can give you."

She turned her attention back to brushing her hair. "What is it you really want, Apollo? I've no time for games today."

He reached out, and clasped her hand, gently bringing it behind her back to press her fingers against his aching member. "I told you, satisfaction."

Her breath quickened, her eyes dark with wanting. The thought of satisfying her baser desires was tempting. God knows, she needed a little release herself. The orgasms she'd experienced moments ago hadn't been enough to curb her body's desires. Yet she knew she couldn't fulfill his request. At least, not yet. She had more pressing matters to attend to, and now was not the time for her to impale herself on a man's cock, much less on Apollo's.

He sensed her arousal, and leaned forward to brush a hand across her bare left shoulder. His fingers slipped beneath the edge of her dress as he moved his hand downward to cup her breast. He raked his nails across her nipple, his penis throbbing painfully. Apollo let go of her arm, and brought his free hand upward to curl his fingers around her chin. He tilted her head back, and bent his head to catch her lips with his. She moaned, allowing him access into her mouth. His tongue plundered its warm depths as his hand plucked and pinched her taut nipple.

Artemis caught herself before he could go any further. She shoved her chair back, causing him to release her and step aside. She pushed herself to her feet, and pulled her clothes back into order. Though her body's hunger was hard to ignore, she left Apollo standing in place, and promptly teleported herself out of her chambers without another word.

CHAPTER 6

"Artemis?" Deivos inquired as he came face-to-face with the beautiful goddess.

She smiled, and stepped out of the shadows, her silvery-yellow eyes appraising his six-foot-seven frame. "Deivos," she breathed. "How good to see you!"

His eyes narrowed as he took in her seductively clad body. Her auburn hair was loosely curled around her shoulders, fluttering gently as she moved about. She now wore a pair of tight black leather pants tucked into thigh-high black leather heeled boots along with an open black sheer blouse settled across her shoulders. Beneath it, a black and red corset hugged her flesh, her ample breasts peeking over its top edge. Gold and silver bracelets clinked around her wrists, and she wore a diamond ring on each of her ring fingers. A gold belt completed the ensemble, hanging low around her waist.

"Gettin' ready to party, eh?"

She chuckled softly, and shook her head. "No. I've

come to see you, actually."

His hazel eyes widened with surprise. "Dressed like that?"

Her smile disappeared. "What's wrong with what I'm wearing?"

"N–Nothin'. It's just . . . Ya don't look like yer dressed for a casual chat, Love. In fact, I 'onestly thought ya were 'eaded to a club or somethin'."

"Oh. Well, no. I'm just here to see you. I was in the mood to feel beautiful and seductive, that's all."

He clasped her hand, and led her over to a settee sitting in the middle of the room. "Well, ya 'ave certainly achieved 'at. 'Ave a seat. Is there anythin' I can get ya?"

She waved her hand about. "I'm fine, thanks. Sit down, Deivos. We need to talk."

A frown marred the beautiful contours of his face. He slid into the leather recliner across from her, prepared for the worst. "What about?"

"Have you found out who she is?"

"Who?"

"The girl in the picture you gave me. Several weeks have passed since you first gave me that photograph, and I've heard nothing else from you. I held off on taking further action because I figured you were hard at work in finding out what I wanted to know. Is that not the case?"

He breathed a sigh of relief. "It . . . Yes, 'at's the case. I've been 'ard at work, yes."

She raised a brow at him. "Well?"

"'Er name is Callidora Spiros."

"*Gift of Beauty*," she mused. "Anything else?"

"No, Milady. All I was able to discover was 'er name. An' 'at was only 'cause I came across 'er at a club the other night. She's quite talkative once she's 'ad a couple drinks under 'er belt."

Artemis frowned. "That's it? All this time, and all you have to show for it is her name? Did you at least think of following her?"

He lowered his eyes as his face grew warm. "I tried."

"But?"

"It's like she disappeared. She got wind of the fact 'at someone was followin' 'er. One minute, she was there, an' the next, she was gone."

Her jaw clenched with effort as she fought to hold back the anger boiling beneath the surface. "Have you seen her since?"

"No. But—"

She raised a hand, and cut him off. "Enough! I expect results, Deivos. If you're to share in the spoils of war, you have to be more efficient."

He looked up at her, his eyes full of curiosity. "Spoils of war? Is she 'at important?"

She leaned forward, exposing her ample cleavage to his view. "Of course, she is. Why else would I have you find out more about her?"

He fidgeted uncomfortably, adjusting his pants as they tightened across his crotch. "I assumed she was just a passin' fancy of yers."

She smirked, and shook her head. "Hardly. I'm the protector of young girls, Deivos. Her safety has been in question ever since you brought her to my attention."

He swallowed audibly as his face paled. "Someone's after 'er?"

"Yes, and I want to make sure no harm comes to her," she lied smoothly. "Which is why you need to work harder in finding out everything you can about her. Where she lives, who she stays with, and what she does during the day or night. Anything and everything about her must be accounted for. Is that understood?"

He withered beneath her intense scrutiny. "Yes, Milady. I will do my best."

She stood, smoothing out the imaginary wrinkles on her sheer blouse. "You do that," she replied, and orbed herself out of his living room, leaving him alone to contemplate as to whether their conversation had ever happened in the first place.

CHAPTER 7

A myriad of thoughts spun through Artemis' mind as she walked along Sixth Avenue. She'd given Deivos the task of finding out everything possible about Callidora Spiros, but her curiosity in regards to the girl would not let up. Thus, she'd done a little digging of her own, and had come across the address leading to the girl's work place.

She stopped in front of the small boutique, and pretended to window shop, discreetly taking a look inside. A raven-haired beauty lounged against a counter, her cornflower blue eyes focused on something Artemis couldn't see. She surmised that the young woman was approximately the same height as she, five-feet-eight inches tall. Though, she could have been wrong, as the girl was wearing a pair of black stilettos.

She was tempted to march inside, and pluck the chit out of the store to take her back to Mount Olympus. Yet she knew she couldn't. Without the proper information at her disposal, there was no telling as to whether her current prey really was the *Child of Calamity*. Though the prophecy spoke avidly of the *Harbinger of Chaos and Destruction*, there was no mention of what the child looked like. Nor would anyone know as to whom the being in question would be born to. All she had were her assumptions. The girl was tied to the pantheon itself, but she wasn't sure of what those exact ties were. Not yet, anyway.

A sharp gasp broke past her lips as she turned around, and bumped into the last person she expected to see. "Hades!"

He smiled down at her, his dark-brown eyes shining with amusement. "Beautiful, isn't it?"

"What is?"

He pointed to the dress in the window. "The dress. You should try it on."

She turned in the direction he was facing. Where moments ago there hadn't been anything, a silvery-yellow strapless dress now adorned a delicate-looking mannequin. She gasped with astonishment as the dress took on a different form before her very eyes.

Gold and green leaves spread across the bodice's border, inching toward its seam, and down to its hem. Interspersed with the leaves, were the images of a huntress holding a bow and arrow as numerous animals crowded around her. The ivy moved upward, and came to a stop at the V-shape holding the bodice and flared skirt together. The dress was beautiful, and she found herself wanting it all the more.

"Y–You did that!?"

Hades grinned. "Of course. Go on in. Try it on."

"But . . ."

"You know you want to, so I'm giving you the opportunity you seek. Consider this a gift, though it comes with a warning. The girl must not come to harm. None. At all. Is that understood?"

She frowned. "How did you . . . ?"

His eyes gleamed with suppressed menace. "I have my ways. You're not the only one searching for answers, Artemis. You must hurry. Time is of the essence, so make use of it!"

He disappeared, leaving her alone. Several passersby stared at her with perplexion as she mumbled to herself. She ignored their curious looks, and cursed her uncle for being so astute. She should have known that he'd dig further into the situation at hand. The fact that he'd deduced what her next course of action might have been also disturbed her. Yet she chose not to think about that fact for the time being. She gathered a hold of her composure, took a deep breath, and strode into the shop.

***

"May I help you?" Callidora Spiros inquired as Artemis stepped inside.

She plastered a timid smile upon her lips, and nodded. "Yes," she said, her voice a tad breathless. She pointed to the dress Hades had fashioned for her as it sat in the adjacent window. "I'd like that dress."

Callidora's gaze swung toward the mannequin she pointed to. "You've good taste. That dress is made by Herbert Underland."

Artemis stifled a laugh, and feigned ignorance. *I'm so going to give my uncle hell about that later!* "Who?"

Callidora rolled her eyes, and waved her hand about in dismissal. "You're kidding, right?"

"Umm . . . no."

She walked over to the mannequin, and gently tugged it down. "Herbert Underland is THE man of the hour. His fashion designs are found all over the world. As you can see, he uses the finest silks. The embroidery is to die for!"

Callidora spoke as if she'd known about Hades her entire life, yet such a fact was impossible. Her uncle had created the garment at a moment's notice.

No, she thought. *Hades must have placed such thoughts in her head to make the dress's creation more credible.*

The girl plucked the dress off of the mannequin, and held it up to the light. "Sadly, his creations are expensive as hell."

"You own some?"

"Gosh, no. I wish."

Artemis' gaze was drawn to the garment once more. "It's a beautiful dress. Quite exquisite, if I may say so."

Callidora smiled softly, and ran her finger along the dress's seam. "Yes, it is. The careful craftsmanship he employs on each item he makes is amazing."

Goodness, Uncle. Was it really necessary to alter her mind so much? she thought.

She kept her thoughts in check, and said, "I've never seen such fashion before, in all honesty."

"You should check him out on the internet. He's got a lot of stuff available. Most are already ready-to-wear."

The internet? Dear God, what is that?

"Umm . . . yeah. Sure."

"The color of the dress seems to suit you. It matches the color of your eyes."

Artemis smiled, her eyes gleaming. "It would look great on you, too," she commented casually. "You've the body for it."

A small smile danced across Callidora's lips. "It is beautiful, but . . ."

"But . . . ?"

She sighed dramatically. "I can't afford a dress like this."

Artemis assessed her from head to toe. She wore designer clothes and shoes, exuding an air of refinement. The fact that she was properly bred was obvious, yet she was working at a station that seemed quite beneath her.

Odd, she thought.

"Is it really that expensive?"

Callidora nodded. "A bit."

"I think I'll take it anyway."

"You won't regret it," Callidora replied, slipping the dress into Artemis' waiting hands.

Artemis glanced down at the delicate fabric, admiring her uncle's handiwork. The dress was beautiful. Hades had given her the means in which to meet Callidora. She was grateful to him for giving her the opportunity, yet she could not deny that he didn't trust in her completely. Though he was not aware of it, the girl was a vital part of her plans. She'd gain a small foothold in the scheme of things if she were able to bring the girl onto her team. The question was, how was she going to do that if she barely knew the young woman to begin with?

She cleared her mind, and followed Callidora over to the cash register, producing a wallet with a quick flick of her hand. The girl's eyes widened, but she kept quiet as her eyes focused on the money Artemis had stashed within the leather's folds. The goddess pretended to riffle through the wad of cash.

"How much do I owe you?"

Callidora cleared her throat, and glanced down at the register's screen. "Twenty-five hundred."

"That's it?"

"You want it to be more?"

"Well . . . You said this guy's pieces were expensive."

"With the meager earnings I earn, they are."

"Meager earnings? You don't quite fit in here, in all honesty," she murmured offhandedly.

Callidora looked away, avoiding her intense scrutiny. "Yeah, I get that a lot."

Artemis wanted to place a gentle hand on the girl's shoulder, to comfort her somehow. Yet that sort of thing would not be welcome, most especially since she'd just met the girl.

"I see."

A soft sigh escaped Callidora's lips. "Shall I finish ringing you up?"

The bright sheen of moisture in the girl's eyes wasn't lost on Artemis. The young woman was hiding something, she was sure of it. Curiosity got the best of her, but she tamped the urge to find out as much as possible about Callidora down. The questions she wanted to ask would have to wait. Now was not the time or place for her to indulge in such things.

Instead, she said, "Sure."

She handed over the necessary amount, unaware of the surprised looks in her direction from several customers lounging nearby. Callidora's fingers flew across the register's interface, and she quickly rang up Artemis' purchase. She accepted the bag, change, and receipt once she'd completed the transaction.

"Thank you," she murmured as she slipped the money and the piece of paper into the left pocket of her tight leather pants. She turned around, intent on leaving, when Callidora's voice reached out to her.

"Thanks for stopping by. I hope you like the dress."

Artemis smiled, her eyes alight with pleasure. She composed herself as she whirled about, and nodded. "I do. Thanks again!"

Without another word, she walked out of the boutique, clutching the paper bag tightly between her fingers. It took every ounce of willpower for her not to turn around, and walk right back to further engage Callidora. With a quick flick of her hand, she sent the bag back to the store with Callidora's name on it, and a note tucked within its depths. She lamented the fact that she wasn't keeping the dress, but the girl's curiosity would get the best of her when the time came. Sooner or later, she would seek Artemis out.

She continued walking, her mind focused on the events that had taken place not too long ago. Something about the young woman drew her attention. She wanted to obtain her complete confidence, something she so clearly needed when the time came to gain her acquiescence. One way or another, she would have her allegiance. Only then, would she be able to put her plans into motion, once and for all.

CHAPTER 8

"You seem to be in good spirits," Hades commented as he appeared, and fell into step beside Artemis.

She smiled. "Yes, and I have you to thank for that, Uncle."

"All went well, then?"

She stopped in her tracks, and turned to face him. "Yes," she said. "Quite well."

He ran a hand through his dark-brown curls, a knowing smirk upon his lips. "That's good, I suppose. You didn't buy the dress, though."

"I did."

He quirked a brow at her. "But . . . ?"

She looked down momentarily, and wrung her hands together. "Callidora admired it, too. I thought it would look better on her since she has the body for it. After our impromptu meeting, I sent it back to the store with a means for her to find it."

Hades stared down the bridge of his nose at her. For

a moment, it looked as though he'd crossed his eyes. The intensity of his gaze made her shift uncomfortably. She should have averted her gaze, but her pride refused to allow her to do so. If she was to remain strong and self-sufficient, she needed to show everyone around her that she did, indeed, possess those qualities.

"Why do I have a feeling that you didn't do so out of the kindness of your own heart?"

Her eyes widened with mock horror. "How can you say such a thing, Uncle?"

"As I said once before, your hunting comes with unwanted benefits. I'm still not convinced that your interest in this mortal is pure of heart."

Her lips pursed with displeasure. "If that's the case, then why did you help me?"

"Curiosity got the best of me. Why are you drawn to this girl so much?"

"She intrigues me. Her innocent qualities make me want to protect her all the more. Surely, you know I won't hurt her?"

He crossed his arms upon his chest, his head tilted slightly to the side in contemplation. "I'm not a hundred percent sure on that yet. Perhaps you'd like to enlighten me?"

Her pulse raced as she realized he was fishing for answers. Answers she could not give him. Though Hades was her favorite uncle, he would thwart her plans in a heartbeat. Most especially if he were to become privy to the fact that they involved taking over Mount Olympus. Every god and goddess coveted the golden throne. Many had tried to take it from her father, but none had succeeded in doing so.

She, on the other hand, was determined to make it hers, once and for all. Her duplicity was to be one that no one would see coming. Well, if Apollo made sure to keep his mouth shut, anyway. She still needed to silence him on that account. The question was, how?

The sound of Hades' clearing his throat brought her out of her reverie. "What?" she prodded, a slight frown marring the center of her forehead.

"I'm still curious as to why the girl intrigues you."

"She's family."

"Are you sure?"

"Why wouldn't she be?"

The left corner of Hades' mouth tilted upward with amusement. "Perhaps you should dig a little deeper, and get your facts straight, Artemis. What if she really is a mortal? What then?"

She stared back at him, appalled. "There's no way she could be, Uncle. She's too well-protected."

"Some humans can afford to be. The girl obviously has money, so . . ."

Her frown deepened. She'd noticed Callidora's designer clothes and her air of refinement from the get-go. Yet the girl had tried to play things off as if they were nothing. She was hiding who she was for a reason.

But why? she wondered. *Can it really be so simple?*

She straightened to her full height of five-feet-eight, and focused her eyes on her uncle. "Why are you really here?"

Hades spread his arms wide, feigning innocence. "I came to see how things went for you. Nothing more."

The hairs on the back of Artemis' neck stood on end. He purposefully kept something from her. She could sense it. "What aren't you telling me?"

"Nothing you already know, dear. I want to make sure that the girl comes to no harm."

"Why?"

"Let's just say I now have a vested interest in the situation."

"Such as?"

His dark eyes bored into hers. "Such as, I'm keeping my eyes on you. Be careful of where you tread. Not everyone will give you the helping hand you seek."

He disappeared, leaving her alone to ponder his words. She became cognizant of the fact that her uncle understood more about the situation than he let on. Deciphering exactly what he knew was another matter entirely, however. He was good at keeping secrets just like she was. She needed to uncover Hades' secrets if she was to remain one step ahead of him. To do that, she needed to seek out the one person she never thought of seeing so soon–the beautiful and enigmatic Persephone.

CHAPTER 9

Artemis closed her eyes, and took a deep breath to steady herself, oblivious of the world around her. In the blink of an eye, she found herself in the middle of Persephone's chambers on Mount Olympus. Unfortunately, she was not alone. Hades was with her. His presence in the room was a stark contrast to his usual place in Tartarus. The pair turned to face her. A knowing look flashed across Hades' face, while annoyance clouded Persephone's delicate features.

"What are you doing here?" Hades inquired as he handed his wife a white silk dress.

"How did you get here so quickly?" Artemis shifted uncomfortably beneath her uncle's sharp gaze.

"I'm a god, Artemis. We travel faster than the speed of light. You know that as well as I do. Is there something you want?"

"I came to see Persephone."

"In regards to?"

"Something."

A glint of menace danced in Hades' eyes. "Such as?"

She airily flicked a hand about. "It's a woman's thing. You wouldn't understand."

"You'd be surprised as to what my husband understands," Persephone said as she accepted the dress he handed her. "Is it dire?"

"Is what dire?"

Persephone assessed her from head to toe, and shook her head. "Your problem. Because if it's not, I don't have time to address it right now."

Artemis' eyes widened as she glanced about. She realized, then, what Persephone was doing. "You're packing!"

"Yes, I am."

"But . . . Why? You're not due to go back to Tartarus yet."

Her aunt glanced at her husband, and smiled. "I'm heading home several days early."

"Won't that disrupt the balance of seasons?"

"It just means that winter comes a little early this year, that's all. I miss my home, Artemis. Surely, you can understand that?"

"Well, yes, but . . ."

Hades dropped the bundle of clothes he was now holding, and came to stand in front of her. His dark eyes bored into hers. "Why are you here?"

"I told you, I need to—"

"Talk to my wife, yes. I got that already. About what?"

A muscle twitched along her jaw as Artemis clenched her teeth tight with frustration. "It's personal."

Her uncle chuckled. "I know all about women's ailments, dear. Now don't be shy. Tell us what's wrong."

She stared at him, looking appalled. "N–No!" she cried, and orbed herself out of Persephone's quarters.

Artemis soon found herself in the middle of her own room. She began to pace back and forth, angrily tugging at her auburn curls as she mumbled to herself. Hades must have known she'd seek Persephone out.

But how? she wondered. *How is it that he's one step ahead of me?*

A swift knock upon her door drew her attention. "Who is it?"

"It's Nephele, Milady," the voice replied.

"Yes?"

The doors opened, and a petite blonde strode inside. Her hazel eyes swept across the room with appreciation. "Is there something you require?"

"No."

The girl nodded, and turned around, intent on leaving.

"Wait!"

Nephele faced Artemis once more, an expression of adoration spreading across her face as she stared at her beloved goddess. "Yes, Mistress?"

Artemis hurried to the desk sitting to the left of her bed, and scrawled a short message across a piece of parchment. She folded it thrice, and heated a piece of red wax. With precise movements, she stamped her sigil, a bow and arrow sitting upon a lunar disk, in the middle to seal the letter closed. She turned around, and made her way over to her handmaiden. With a flick of her hand, she slipped the parchment into the girl's hands.

"I need you to deliver that to my brother, Apollo."

Nephele glanced at the letter. "Yes, Milady. As you wish."

A deep frown marred her forehead as she waited for the girl to fulfill her request. Frustration boiled up within her as Nephele remained where she was standing. Minutes passed, and still, she did not move. Instead, her eyes were drawn to Artemis' taut form.

"Well?"

"Yes, Mistress?"

"Aren't you going to do as I have asked of you?"

Embarrassed, Nephele glanced at her sandal clad feet. "Must you not dismiss me?"

Artemis' cheeks flushed a deep red color. "Oh. Yes! You're dismissed."

The girl curtsied before her, and hurried toward the open door. She murmured a quick, "Thank you," as the door swung closed.

A soft sigh slid past her lips as she surveyed her surroundings. Nothing was going as planned. She'd made a small headway in regards to Callidora, but it was not enough to get things to where they needed to be.

She turned on the balls of her feet, and made her way toward the balcony, overlooking the expansive gardens below. Though she was not yet close to achieving her goals, she was confident everything would come together soon enough. Granted, she'd encountered a bit of opposition, thus far, but none of it had deterred her plans as of yet.

Hades and Apollo's involvement in the scheme of things needed to be addressed. She had to make sure they were both on her side. Apollo could be taken care of easily. Hades, on the other hand, was another matter entirely. Never-the-less, she was determined to gain the upper hand, at all cost. The battle for Mount Olympus depended on it.

CHAPTER 10

Knowing that it would be awhile before Apollo made his appearance, Artemis decided to seek a little entertainment. She strode out of her room, and walked down the brightly lit corridor. Her mind was full of turmoil as she thought about the plans she'd set into motion.

She wanted everything to be perfect for when the time came for her to take over the throne. Callidora was one of her father's illegitimate children. She was sure of it. The woman protecting the girl was certainly beautiful. She wasn't quite sure if she was the girl's real mother, but she'd find out soon enough.

The *Child of Calamity* was an avid part of her plan. Once her father was made aware of her existence, he'd do everything possible to keep her a secret. Each and every god and goddess coveted the lore behind the prophecy itself. Though the child's gender or name was unknown, the thought of having such power at their disposal was something everyone wanted.

Except Zeus. Her father often claimed that the prophecy was a lie. That it was created to ensure that Mount Olympus was ruled with an iron thumb. Yet it is known that behind every lie, there is always a truth. She was convinced she'd found it. Aside from those who were avidly carrying out her wishes, no one else was truly privy to the child's existence.

Aside from Hades, she mused. *I've a feeling he knows more than he's letting on. Why he's keeping things a secret, I do not know.*

Artemis sauntered into the main courtyard of her home, and came to a complete stop. Deivos sat on a wooden bench beneath her favorite willow tree, his shoulder-length brown hair fluttering softly in the breeze. Her nipples hardened as his hazel eyes roved over her now casually clad body. Her mouth grew dry as their gazes clashed, and she saw the hunger burning in his eyes.

She gathered her composure, and said, "What are you doing here?"

A knowing smile played about the demigod's lips. "Ya tol' me to keep an eye on the girl."

"Yes, and?"

"I've news."

She crossed her arms upon her ample breasts. "Go on."

"I've found 'er. Where she works, sleeps, who she 'angs wit'."

Artemis chuckled, and flicked her right hand in the air in dismissal. "I found her place of work not too long ago. Though, her home address will come in handy. Have you found out anything in regards to her mother?"

"No."

"Her father? Is it Zeus?"

"I'm not sure."

She frowned. "Then what am I paying you for?

"Payin' me?" he balked. "Ya call romps in my bed payments? Please, 'at's barely scratchin' the itch between my balls. Ya ain't paid me shite, Artemis, an' ya know it."

Her mouth dropped open with surprise. "How dare you . . . ?"

Deivos stood up, pulling himself up to his full height. He towered over her, his eyes glinting with anger. "I dare, Goddess, 'cause I'm tired of bein' ya lackey. 'Ell, I'm tired of bein' your boy-toy, too. I don't mind doin' ya favors if it benefits me, but this shite wit' the girl . . . . It's gettin' old."

She curled her fingers into tight fists, her eyes blazing with fury. "No one," she breathed, "speaks to me like that!"

He snorted with derision. "I'm not afraid of ya, dearest cousin. I've gone through enough shite wit' ya to know when yer jus' 'ot air."

Though she was not prone to using the elements to her advantage, Artemis was determined in teaching him a lesson. She gathered the particles of water hovering in the air above as Poseidon had taught her to do, and willed them into a full-blown storm. Water pelted them from every direction, the brunt of the storm centered upon Deivos. Lightning crackled above him as she wove several wards in the air with quick jerks of her hands.

His eyes widened as a lightning bolt struck him dead center in the chest. The electricity passed through him, and was absorbed into the ground. He had no chance of regaining his composure before roots and vines exploded from the ground, pinning his soaked body in place. The wind picked up, whipping his sopping wet hair into his eyes. He roared with anger, pleading with Artemis to cease her attack, but the force of the elements continued to batter him left and right. Whatever spell she'd cast had made his ability to teleport useless.

She grinned broadly as she lifted her hands in front of her, and a small vortex of fire spread between her fingers. She sensed his distress, and saw the horror plastered across his face. The thought of marring his perfect complexion tugged at her heartstrings, but she needed to teach him a lesson. One that would remind him of his place when it came to doing her bidding.

In the blink of an eye, the water, lightning, roots, and vines disappeared before she had a chance of tossing the ball of flame in his direction. She swore with vehemence, and tried to call up the elements once more, but something prevented her from doing so. A quick tap on her shoulder soon drew her attention. Her eyes widened as she whirled around to face her father.

"What are you doin'?" he asked, his stormy blue eyes narrowed slightly.

Her chin rose with determination. "Having a lover's spat, Daddy dearest."

"Since when do you use the elements with such

carelessness? I didn't show you how to use my lightnin' bolts 'at way." He looked at Deivos, and nodded. "You may go."

"But I'm not finished with him!"

"You are now," Zeus replied as his nephew regained his powers, and teleported to safety. "Seriously, girl, what are you thinkin'? What would Demeter think if she were to have seen you abuse the earth in such a manner? Poseidon would be appalled to see you use his precious water with such careless abandonment. I'm willing to bet that Hephaestus didn't teach you how to wield fire against another like that. And pray tell, which of the Anemoi taught you how to summon the winds? Hmmm? What's wrong with you?"

Artemis' eyes filled with tears as her father brought her down to size. She'd only wanted to teach Deivos a lesson, to put him in his rightful place. To exert her power over him just enough to make him understand that her wish was his command. In her mind, she wouldn't have hurt him that much. Her orders were meant to be followed. Yet her father had conveniently thwarted her plans.

"I . . ."

"You what?"

"I only meant to scare him," she said, blinking rapidly to keep her tears from falling.

Zeus approached her, and clasped her hands in his. His stern expression softened as he gazed into her eyes. "You've my temperament, dearest. I was just as rash at your age, but you need to curb those impulses. We are gods and goddesses, and are meant to rule over mortals. Yes, we have our own feuds amongst family here, but we do not hurt each other the way you've tried to hurt Deivos. Poseidon would take offense to your hurtin' his offspring. I know I would."

"But—"

"Can it, Lovely. I don't want to hear it. Whatever you did to dampen my nephew's abilities, I suggest you refrain from doin' so again. To anyone. I created you, Artemis. I can take your life without thinkin' twice. We are mighty, but we can still fall. Remember 'at when you try to hurt someone in the future."

He disappeared without another word, leaving her alone in the middle of her courtyard. Puddles of water surrounded her, and her clothes were stuck to her skin. Yet she took no notice of any of it. Her mind reeled with the lecture her father had given her. He'd put her in her place, though he had no clue as to what she planned for him.

She bristled with anger at the fact that he'd threatened to take her life if she stepped out of bounds once more. Deep inside, she refused to let him do so. She loved her life, as well as every aspect of what being the *Goddess of the Hunt* entailed. She would not let her father take her livelihood from her. Nor would she bend to his will or anyone else's. She had the right to live her life the way she wanted to live it. No one was going to take it from her. Not even Zeus.

CHAPTER 11

Artemis closed her eyes, and orbed herself back to her bedroom. She summoned her half-brother, Hermes, as she moved about the room. He appeared before her with his golden crown askew, and his chiton completely wrinkled. His severe disarray was appalling, as was the stench of sex that poured off of him. So much so, that she now regretted calling him forth.

His blue eyes were dilated, and spittle dripped down his chin. "You rang?" he quipped as he swayed back and forth.

"Yes, I did, but it looks like I've caught you at a bad time."

He laughed, and shook his head to clear it. "No, no. I'm ok."

"Are you?" she asked as she took a step back to assess him.

He stumbled toward the chaise lounge in the upper left corner of the room, and dropped his five-foot-eleven frame onto it. "I'm fine. What's up?"

Artemis frowned, and chewed on the tip of a fingernail. "I was hoping you could assist me, but I'm no longer sure if it's a good idea."

"Why not?"

"You're drunk!"

"Psssh! This? I'm a god, Sis. I can warp myself out of a hangover."

She raised a brow at him. "Can you?"

He grinned. "Oh, yeah."

"Prove it."

His smiled disappeared. "What?"

"You heard me. Prove it."

Hermes' blue eyes focused on her face as he did his best to hold himself upright. Apparently, he hadn't expected her to call his bluff. His lips thinned to a tight line. He clutched the edge of the chair between his fingers, closed his eyes, and began to concentrate. She took another step back as he began to glow.

A soft hum vibrated throughout the room as the glow surrounding Hermes grew stronger. Artemis had called his bluff, but she'd never expected him to act upon it. She thought he was kidding about his making the effects of his hangover dissipate. The hum intensified as the light completely enveloped her brother's bulky frame. A soft gasp escaped her as the tumescent glow shot outward. She closed her eyes to shield them from the unexpected luminescence.

Several minutes passed before the room returned to normal. She stood up straight, and opened her eyes to find a smug-looking Hermes sitting before her. The scent of alcohol and sex were gone, as were the effects of his inebriation. He sat in front of her, looking as good as new.

"Holy hell!" he breathed.

"What?"

"I never knew I could do that."

"Do what? Become the world's biggest fireball?"

He glared at her momentarily. "Getting rid of a hangover. I lied about that. But damn! That fucking rocked!"

She chuckled softly, and shook her head. "I bet."

"So what did you want me for?"

Artemis pulled a chair over to him, and promptly sat down. She settled the skirt of her dress across her knees, and said, "I need you to keep an eye on Zeus."

"Come again?"

"I said—"

He cut her off with a quick jerk of his head. "You want me to spy on Zeus?"

"Well, no."

"But you just said . . ."

"That I want you to keep an eye on Zeus."

"That's spying."

"No, it's not."

"Yes, it is!"

She clenched her hands into tight fists. It dawned on her that she'd misjudged him. Deep inside, she'd prayed that he'd give up on his allegiance to their father. That he'd help her with anything necessary. How wrong she'd been. Hermes would lay his sword at her father's feet if it meant he'd get ahead in the scheme of things.

"It's not exactly spying, per se," she stated, moments later.

He crossed his arms upon his chest, his eyes full of suspicion. "How so? What's Father done that requires such secrecy?"

"I . . . I'm not sure."

"You don't know?"

"Yes."

"So, let me get this straight. You want me to keep an eye on Dad's every move, but you can't tell me why?"

She nodded, keeping her face impassive. "Uh-huh."

His eyes widened as a light bulb went off inside his head. "It . . . Does this have to do with that picture Apollo showed me?"

The sound of her heart beating thundered loudly in her eardrums. "Sort of."

"Who is she?"

She shrugged nonchalantly. "I honestly can't say."

"But . . . ?"

"I'm pretty sure she's tied to us somehow."

"And?"

"Daddy's used this supposed prophecy to keep us all in line. The girl is one of us. I'm sure of it."

"Is that why you want me to keep tabs on him?"

"Yes."

"What if your plans backfire?"

She smirked at him. "How would they?" she quipped. "You have no idea what they are."

"No, I don't," he agreed. "But you're known as the chaste huntress for a reason, Artemis. You're up to something. Whatever it is, I want in."

"Do you?"

He tilted his head at her in acknowledgment. "Aye."

A smile tugged at the corners of her mouth. The fact that he wanted to help her was unexpected, but welcome. With his trailing their father's every move, they'd glean the needed information from Zeus in no time. Hermes' involvement in her plans would work out to her advantage in more ways than one.

She clapped her hands with delight. "Perfect!"

An amused smile broke out upon his face. "Aren't you going to tell me what your plans are?"

"In due time, yes."

"I see. What now, then?"

"Now," she said as she pushed herself to her feet, and stared down at him, "you get to watch Zeus carefully. If he notices something, or questions you for any reason, you can claim your innocence in not knowing what I'm up to."

"How's that going to work? Zeus isn't stupid."

"I'm well aware of that, Hermes. The less you know right now, brother, the better."

"What if–?"

She cut him off with a quick flick of her hand. "I think we're done for now. How about you head to Daddy's house, and see what's going on there?"

His mouth pursed with displeasure. "Is that your wish?"

"Yes."

"Very well," he said, and disappeared with a resounding pop that echoed off of the room's walls.

CHAPTER 12

Artemis stared at the chaise lounge Hermes had occupied moments ago with bewilderment. She hadn't expected him to agree to things so easily. Never-the-less, she was pleased that he had. It would make things easier in the long run. The fact that she hadn't shared her plans with him would ensure that no one would be privy to them from the get-go. Aside from Apollo, of course.

A sigh of frustration escaped her as she gazed at her surroundings. She'd expected Nephele to return with Apollo's reply in no time at all, yet she was nowhere in sight. She supposed it was because Apollo still inhabited his place amongst the blue skies, but it honestly didn't take so long to deliver a wretched letter.

Artemis cracked her knuckles with impatience, and strode toward the door of her bedroom. She yanked it open, and shouted down the hall for another attendant. Iokaste and Amynta, two of her handmaidens appeared, moments later. Flustered, they catered to her demands, and set about in preparing another bath for her. Artemis watched as they moved about the room, speaking amongst themselves as they finished putting everything together.

Standing near the bathtub, the women waited for further instructions. Artemis stood, and walked in their direction, calmly waiting for them to help her undress. They stepped forward, and quickly divested her of her garments. She smiled, and thanked them before slipping into the porcelain tub. She then dismissed them with a flick of her hand.

Her body sank into the warm water as the door latched closed behind them. She allowed herself to relax, enjoying the warmth that now covered her every limb. The scent of roses, jasmine, and gardenia wafting into the air soothed her frazzled nerves. The last few days–heck, weeks, had taken their toll on her, and she was beginning to feel the weariness spreading throughout her entire body.

She enjoyed these moments of respite, as they allowed her to make better sense of the world she lived in. Granted, life as a goddess was hectic, at best. There was always something, or someone, drawing her attention. Mortals, most of all, sought her out whenever possible, entreating her to a multitude of requests they hoped she'd help them with. They lived for the blessings she bestowed upon them, while she, in turn, basked in their adoration.

She loved her life, and wouldn't change things for the world. Yet there were times she wanted more. She hated living in other people's shadows, most especially her father's. Zeus ruled Mount Olympus as he saw fit, and dished out punishments accordingly. If something wasn't to his liking, he changed the circumstances until they suited him in every way. He was the king, and every god and goddess knew it. They followed his every rule to the letter, though there were a good many things the gods and goddesses could get away with before Zeus demanded order.

Artemis wanted that power. She wanted her family and friends to revere her, to lay their glory at her feet. She dreamed of the moment when she didn't have to answer to anyone but herself. The thought of living under her father's rule annoyed her, as did the restrictions he imposed on her and the rest of the pantheon.

She aimed to change things once she achieved her goal. Zeus would not be happy, she knew. He loved the power he exerted over her and the rest of her peers. She planned to put Hera in her place as well. That woman had far too much power. Power, she realized, she could use to her advantage.

Artemis settled back against the edge of the tub, and smiled as she thought about the changes she'd put into motion soon enough. She didn't care about the fact that she was being selfish. For once, she was thinking about herself and no one else. Opposition was sure to come from every direction, but she would meet it head-on when the time came. Come what may, she'd reap the fruits of her labor in more ways than one.

CHAPTER 13

Artemis sat up abruptly as a cold mist surrounded her. Some of the now lukewarm water spilled onto the floor. She wrapped her arms around her upper body, her eyes widening with horror as she watched the walls of her home dissolve. The cream-colored walls were soon replaced with an aqua-colored marble. Her heart hammered within her chest as she realized she was now in her uncle's domain.

A door opened to her left, and Poseidon himself strode into the room. She slipped lower into the water, keeping her arms wrapped around her heaving bosom. Her uncle stared down at her, his stormy blue eyes dark with an emotion she could not name.

"Uncle!" she said.

The corners of Poseidon's mouth twitched with amusement. "Artemis," he replied as he snapped his fingers in front of him.

A chair materialized in thin air, and gently floated to

the floor. He sat down, and crossed one leg upon the other. The door swung open, and a slew of servants hurried inside. They set about in preparing a table Artemis hadn't taken notice of when she'd appeared in her uncle's quarters. They spoke softly amongst themselves, sending covert glances in her direction as they worked.

Her face flushed with color as she realized what they must have been thinking. She was naked, and sitting in a tub full of water in front of Poseidon. To them, it didn't matter that they were family. All they saw was a man and a woman in what looked like a compromising position. It didn't matter that things between them were completely innocent.

She frowned, and turned her attention back to Poseidon. "What am I doing here?"

"We need to talk."

"You could have come to Mount Olympus."

He rolled his eyes, and shook his head. Several blond locks fell across his brow. He cleared his throat, and dismissed his servants with a quick jerk of his head. They filed out of the room in a single line, the door swinging softly closed behind them.

"I prefer to conduct business here, away from my brother's prying eyes."

"You fear Zeus?"

"Who doesn't? I don't exactly fear him, per se. I like my privacy, that's all. This," he waved his arms about, "suits my purposes perfectly."

Goosebumps erupted all over her flesh as she

became cognizant of the rapidly cooling water. "You could have sent word, Uncle. I'd have come better prepared."

"Where's the fun in that?"

He pushed himself to his feet, and walked toward the massive bed to the right of him. He picked up the white sheer fabric strewn across the bed, staring at the garment with appreciation. A knowing smile spread across his lips as he set it down once more.

"Why don't you get dressed?"

"With what? My things are back on Mount Olympus."

He pointed to the articles of clothing lying on the bed. "These are for you."

"But . . ."

"How did I know?"

"Yes."

He walked over to her, and knelt beside the bathtub. He dipped a finger into the cooling water, and smiled. "I am the ruler of the seas, Artemis. The water belongs to me. I'm well aware of everything and everyone who sets foot in it. Be it on land or sea. I'm always aware when you or any of my brethren partake of such cleansing rituals."

"But you've never . . ."

"Overstepped my boundaries?" She nodded. "I've never had to. This time, however, was a necessity. You and I have some unfinished business."

"Can I at least get some privacy?"

He stood up, and took a step back. "Of course."

Her frown deepened. "Can you leave?"

"I think not, but I will accord you the privacy you so desire." A thick terry towel materialized in his hands. He gently placed it across the tub's edge, and turned his back on her. "You may proceed."

Growling with frustration, she grabbed the towel, and stood up. Rivulets of water cascaded off of her skin in every direction. She wrapped the thick cloth around her slender frame, and stepped out of the tub. She marched toward her uncle's bed, and stared at the clothing he'd assembled for her. The sheer fabric of the dress was not something she usually wore. Unfortunately, there was nothing else for her to wear. She could have summoned something more appropriate, but she had a feeling it wouldn't be to Poseidon's liking.

With a sigh of discontent sliding past her lips, she allowed the towel to drop to the floor. She felt her uncle's eyes pinned on her back as she moved forward to dress. Artemis grabbed the thin silk undergarments, and slipped her legs into them, quickly pulling them up. She fastened the white brassiere across her breasts, and slid the dress over her head. A pair of golden sandals appeared on her dainty feet.

She turned around to face Poseidon. "Well?"

He smiled, and whistled with appreciation. "Beautiful." He held out his hand, and waited for her to take it. "Shall we?"

She stared at his extended appendage. "What?"

He inclined his head toward the table laden with all sorts of fruits, cheeses, meats, drinks, and a myriad of assorted dishes. "I've had dinner prepared for you."

She raised a brow at him. "Have you been spying on me?"

His smiled broadened as she accepted his hand. "Perhaps." He led her toward the table, and pulled out a chair for her.

She sat down, and gingerly smoothed the dress's skirt around her knees. "Thanks," she said as he made his way to the other side of the table, and sat down.

Artemis stared at her uncle, trying to make sense of the current turn of events. She was unable to fathom as to why he'd brought her to Aegae. There was nothing of importance for them to discuss. Granted, she'd mentioned the *Child of Calamity* to him not too long ago. She hadn't revealed too much about what she knew of the girl to him. Had she?

Poseidon cleared his throat, and drew her attention to him. "You're wondering as to why I've brought you here."

"Yes."

"Do you recall our previous conversation?"

"The one in the gardens back home?"

"That's the one."

"What about it?"

He reached out, and grabbed a plate, filling it with several fruits, cheeses, and rolled meats. His eyes bored into her as he plucked a grape, and shoved it between his lips. "You required a favor in exchange for telling me a little more about the *Child of Calamity*."

"I remember that, yes."

He leaned forward in his chair, the look on his face

unreadable. "I did a little digging of my own."

Her pulse thundered in her ears. "And?"

He snapped his fingers, and a piece of paper materialized nearby. Her mouth grew dry as she watched it flutter to the table in front of her. She gazed at the very picture she'd shown Apollo several days ago.

"You recognize it."

"Yes."

"Who is she?"

She looked at him, perplexed. "You don't know?"

"I'd like you to tell me."

"Uncle . . ."

He crossed his arms upon the table's edge. "What do you want her for?"

"N–Nothing!"

His eyes narrowed. "You're lying."

"Am I?"

"You never do things without having a solid reason, Artemis. Why does this woman intrigue you so? The girl is nothing. She's not even one of us."

Artemis snapped out of her stupor, and sat up straight. "She's not?"

"The young woman is human. She does not possess any qualities that would mark her as a demigoddess."

"You're not sure about that, are you?" she prodded, amused. "That's why you're plugging me for answers."

His face blanched. He hadn't expected her to catch on so quickly. "Perhaps," he murmured, deftly pulling himself together. "Why do you believe she's the *Child of Calamity*?"

She shrugged nonchalantly. "Instincts. She's tied to us. I can sense it."

He leaned back against his chair. "That's all you have to go on? Your gut's feelings?"

She pushed herself to her feet, angrily staring down at Poseidon. "Perhaps, but it's all I've got right now."

"You know who she is, don't you?"

"Maybe. I'm guessing you already have the answers you seek, Uncle, which means you never needed to see me in the first place."

He grinned broadly at her. "Clever girl."

"What do you want?"

"Whatever you're up to, I want in. I'd like to help you."

"Do you?"

"Yes."

Her hackles rose, and her eyes narrowed. "I'll think about it, and get back to you on that, Uncle," she said, and flashed herself home.

CHAPTER 14

The scent of apple blossoms and gardenias assailed Artemis' nose as she reappeared in the middle of her garden. Tears coursed down her cheeks unbidden as she crumpled to the ground. The weight of what she'd set into motion lay heavy upon her shoulders.

In sharing her thoughts about the *Child of Calamity* with Apollo, she'd unleashed a giant can of worms. No one had known about the child's existence until she'd done so. Granted, the child was no longer a child, but rather a fetching nineteen-year-old young woman. One who drew a person's attention everywhere she went. The girl was mortal, but she also possessed the blood of a very powerful god. In Artemis' mind, she belonged to Zeus. Callidora exuded a power unlike any other, even if she wasn't yet aware of it.

Artemis curled up into a tight ball, and pulled her knees up against her chest. She buried her face in the small dip between them. Her body shook as she cried, wishing that she could somehow change the course of some of the actions she'd undertaken, thus far. It upset her that far too many were now privy to Callidora's existence. Such circumstances did not bode well for her plans. She wasn't sure as to how she would be able to fix things.

Her tears subsided, moments later. Artemis uncurled her legs, and lay on her side. She stared at the flowers dipping to and fro in the distance. A small smile spread across her lips as she felt Zephyrus, the *God of the West Wind's*, gentle touch ripple across the exposed flesh of her left shoulder. He materialized before her, his light brown hair blowing gently around his head. His amber eyes were full of kind understanding.

He leaned down, and clasped her hands, carefully pulling her to her feet. Zephyrus helped her over to the bench beneath her favorite willow tree. A soft smile swept across his lips as they sat down. He brushed her tears aside with the pads of his thumbs before patting her hands in reassurance.

"My dearest Artemis," he murmured. "Yer in a pickle, aren't ye?"

She stared down at their intertwined hands as her face grew warm. "Somewhat."

"The winds know yer secrets, dear one."

She looked up, her eyes wide with worry. "My secrets?"

"Aye. Depending on which one of us blows across each new day, the news reaching our ears is nev'r the same. There are tales, Artemis, of the webs ye weave."

Her throat constricted as realization dawned on her. "How far and wide have the rumors gone?"

"Word has gone no further than what I and my brothers have discussed."

"But . . . ?"

"Ye must be careful," Zephyrus replied. "There are those who will not take kindly to what ye have set into motion."

"I know."

"No, dearest, ye don't. Word has a way of getting out."

She worried her lower lip in thought. "Meaning?"

"Be careful as to whom ye trust. There are wolves in sheep's clothing."

"You speak in riddles, Zeph. Why?"

He grinned, though his mirth did not quite reach his eyes. "Because I must. I only came to warn ye. There's treachery afoot, and ye are in the thick of it."

She searched the depths of his eyes for a sign that he was lying. Yet she saw nothing that alluded to that fact. He was telling her the truth. Something, she knew, that came at a great cost. One she hoped he would never have to pay.

"Thank you," she breathed, squeezing his hand.

"Ye risk a good many things, child. I fear for ye."

"You needn't, Zeph. I'll be fine. I thank you and your brothers for guarding my secrets."

"We are good at such things. Ye would be surprised as to the things we've been privy to about the entire pantheon."

She chuckled softly, and shook her head. "I can imagine."

Zephyrus pulled his hands free of hers, and stood up. His gentle look warmed her from within. "Company heads this way. I must go. Remember what I said, Artemis."

"I will," she said as her eyes closed of their own volition.

She felt Zephyrus' light touch blow across her left cheek. He took the soft breeze with him as he said goodbye. Her eyes opened as she heard several clinks of metal rubbing together in the distance. Nephele appeared, moments later, a thin piece of parchment clutched between her fingers. She came to a stop in front of her, and dropped to her knees. Her blond hair lay in subtle disarray around her shoulders.

"You have word from Apollo?" Artemis inquired.

Nephele looked up at her beloved mistress. "Yes."

"Let's hear it."

The girl extended the letter in her direction. She accepted the paper, and quickly broke the seal. She scanned the words hastily scrawled across the vellum's surface. A broad smile spread across her lips. Nephele witnessed her delight, though she had no idea as to what brought it on.

"You may go."

Nephele stood, and executed a perfect curtsy in front of her. "Yes, Milady."

Artemis grabbed her arm as she turned to leave. A small brown bag appeared in the palm of her hand. "This is for the great service you have done for me."

Nephele's hazel eyes opened wide. "You're dismissing me?"

"No. Consider it a gift," Artemis replied. "I have need of you yet."

A sigh of relief escaped the girl's lips. "I . . . Thank you, Mistress."

"Please, call me Artemis."

Nephele swallowed past the lump now forming in her throat. She nodded with understanding, curtsied once more, and hurried out of the garden without a backward glance in Artemis' direction. The goddess chuckled to herself, and shook her head. She reread her brother's note before setting it on fire. The ashes scattered to the winds, taking with them Apollo's words.

Artemis pushed herself to her feet, and breathed a sigh of relief. Zephyrus' words had calmed her down considerably. She was able to make sense of the precariousness of her current situation. Others were now cognizant of the *Child of Calamity's* existence. Though they had no idea as to who she really was, whereas she and Deivos did. She suspected that Hades was well aware of the girl's true origins, but he would never divulge that information. He had his own cards in which to play.

Never-the-less, she had enough information to go on when it came to Callidora Spiros. She'd use it to her advantage. The changes she would instigate were intended to better the state in which the pantheon now found itself in. With Apollo and Hermes' help, she'd take Mount Olympus as her own. It was her due, after all.

She took one last look at her surroundings, and closed her eyes. With a mere thought, she fled the confines of her home. Her heart raced as she anticipated seeing her beloved brother. She couldn't wait to put the rest of her plans into motion. Somehow, some way, everything would come together, and she'd finally make her dreams come true.

CHAPTER 15

"You rang?" Apollo whispered into Artemis' ear as he materialized behind her.

A knowing smile played about her lips as she clutched the Battery Park boardwalk railing. Her eyes raked the horizon. Liberty Island and Ellis Island loomed in the distance. The moment was peaceful, one she enjoyed immensely. Yet she knew the contentment she was feeling would not last long.

She turned around to face her brother, taking in his swollen cheeks and haggard appearance. "What took you long enough?"

He avoided her intense scrutiny, shuffling from foot to foot. "Yeah, umm . . . I was detained."

Her hackles rose, as did her suspicion. "By whom?"

"No one of importance."

"Father summoned you?"

"No."

"Then who?"

He shrugged. "It's no one you need to worry about. At least, not yet."

Her eyes widened with alarm. "What have you done?" she asked, her voice barely a whisper.

"H–Hera," Apollo stammered.

"You told her?"

"No, but she caught me trying to find out more about the girl whose picture you showed me. I recalled it from memory, and made a copy. Hera came to see me, cited something about the sun needing to rise as scheduled. The photograph was in plain view. She demanded I tell her who she was. Her cronies tried to rough me up when I denied having any further knowledge of the girl."

"Did you cave under the pressure?"

"No. I think that's what pissed her off more."

Artemis released a pent-up breath, nervously wringing her hands together. "So my plans . . . They're safe?"

Apollo nodded. "Yes, but I'm not sure for how long. Hera . . ."

"Hera won't stop until she has the information she seeks in the palm of her hand. This means we'll need to be more careful from now on."

"How? That woman can sniff things out from a mile away."

"Not this. Not if you keep quiet."

Apollo's shoulders slumped with defeat. "I don't know, Sis. I'm not good at that. At least, not for long."

Artemis approached him, and curled a hand beneath

his chin. She gently tugged his head up so that they were looking at one another, eye to eye. "You are," she cooed. "You need better discipline, that's all. This will be a good lesson in learning how to achieve it."

He pulled his chin out of her grasp, and ran a hand through his blond hair. "I can never understand your faith in me."

"You're my twin, brother. I'm obligated to have faith in you," she said, chewing on her lower lip in thought. "There is a way to redeem yourself, however."

"How so?"

"Keep an eye on the girl for me."

"How am I going to do that?"

She glared at him, and turned around to face the turbulent waters of the harbor once more. "You're the *God of Light*. You rule the skies as you see fit, as well as see and hear everything below you. Keeping an eye on her will be as easy as making a pie."

He came to stand beside her, his eyes roving over the stormy seas. "What do I get in return?"

A knowing smile played about her lips as she glanced at him out of the corner of her eye. "Me."

"Is that a promise?"

"Yes."

"Then you have a deal."

He dematerialized without uttering another word, leaving her alone to enjoy the beautiful scenery spreading out before her. A soft sigh escaped her lips as she leaned against the railing. So far, things weren't going as planned, but she had faith that they would in the long run.

She'd have the *Child of Calamity* in the palm of her hand soon enough. The prospect pleased her immensely, more than she thought it would. Mount Olympus would be hers. She'd make sure of that, no matter the cost.

Artemis took a deep breath. Her gaze swept across the harbor in front of her one last time before she flashed herself home. There was time enough yet to put the rest of her plans into order. For now, she would kick back, relax, and enjoy the ride for all it was worth.

THE CHILD OF CALAMITY SERIES
BOOK 2

Protected
Secrets

LISSETTE E. MANNING

Sometimes, the past is better left buried.

Upon learning of Artemis' intentions, Hades has vowed to thwart her every plan. He's not sure as to why she's set her sights on the beautiful Callidora Spiros, but he refuses to allow her the upper hand. The gods are treacherous and deceitful, more so when they want something.

Well aware of the prophecy concerning the *Child of Calamity*, he knows it's one Artemis seeks to use to her advantage. Determined to keep the secrets of the past dormant, he'll do everything possible to keep things under wraps. Though he's loath to admit it, he knows that very prophecy can change the world as he knows it.

The lines of battle have been drawn. For his family, he'll do whatever is necessary to keep them safe. There is a reason he's known as the cold and callous *Lord of the Underworld*, a fact he makes known whenever possible. He's come too far to allow the other gods and goddesses to rip apart what he's painstakingly gone to great lengths to protect.

Come what may, he will hold fast to that which he loves the most. No one is going to take them from him. Not even Artemis and Zeus' wretched prophecy.

CHAPTER 1

With a flick of his hand, Hades produced a copy of the photograph Artemis had shown him several hours ago. His dark brown eyes narrowed as he gazed upon the young woman's face. She was beautiful. Her blue-black hair curled gently around her shoulders, her cornflower blue eyes focused on the camera. She was dressed in casual clothes and a portion of her left arm looked as if it was wrapped around a woman's shoulders. He automatically knew who the other woman was without needing to see her face.

How did Artemis come across her? he wondered. *There's no way this could be a coincidence.*

A slight pop in the middle of the room drew his attention. The very woman who occupied his thoughts stood before him, her icy blue eyes trained upon him. He set the image down on top of his desk, and pushed his chair back to stretch his cramped limbs.

"You heeded my summons," he murmured softly.

Medusa pursed her lips and crossed her arms about her chest. "Of course. Why would I not?"

He smirked with amusement. "Considering that we butt heads on occasion, I thought—"

"Oh, please," she said, cutting him off abruptly. "You are my master, Hades. I must do as I am bidden."

"Actually, I'm not."

"No?" she prodded as she made her way over to the plush cushioned chair in front of his desk. She sat down and daintily crossed her legs. Her leather pants tightened across her thighs, drawing his attention. "You saved me from a certain death, gave me a way to live a new life, and have allowed me to do as I please on occasion. I'm indebted to you, therefore you are my master."

He snorted and rolled his eyes. "I beg to differ. I wanted to save you from Athena's wrongful wrath, that's all."

"And you did. For that, dearest Hades, you have my undying loyalty. I'm grateful for everything you and Persephone have done for me and Callidora."

"How is she?"

Medusa absently glanced at her fingernails. "She's fine, I suppose."

"You suppose?"

"She's insistent on making her mark on the world."

He sat down once more, cupping his hands behind his head. "Children are so difficult sometimes, aren't they?"

"Unfortunately." She grimaced and sighed dramatically. "She takes after her father."

"I can imagine. He must be quite proud of her."

She stared intently at him, before smiling with amusement. "I dearly hope so."

"You hope so?"

"Come on now, Hades. You and I are both privy to her true parentage. Why would her father not be proud of her? At nineteen years of age, Callidora is a force to be reckoned with. She not only bears Gorgon blood, but also that of a powerful Greek god. How much more special could she be?"

He assessed her from head to toe, wanting so much to tell her what she wanted to hear. Yet he knew he couldn't. For Persephone's sake, he needed to keep his past a secret. Most especially, when it came to Medusa and her beautiful daughter.

"We've a problem."

"Oh?"

Hades leaned forward in his chair, and picked up the photograph. He examined it once more before handing it to Medusa. She accepted the glossy paper, her brow dipping low across her forehead as she looked at it. Several tears escaped from the corners of her eyes. She wiped them away with her free hand, and looked up to meet his turbulent gaze.

"Where did you get this?"

He intertwined his hands and leaned his chin against them. "It's not the original."

"I can see that. Where did it come from?"

"Artemis."

Her eyes opened wide, fear clouding their depths.

"How?"

"Deivos gave it to her. Or so she said."

She shook her head in denial. "It can't be! He . . . He's been faithful to Alexandros!"

Hades snagged the photograph out of her hands, and glanced at the demigoddess's face. "Everyone's loyalty can be purchased for a price. Perhaps my niece offered him something of great value. Whatever it is, it was an offer he couldn't refuse."

"As the *God of Wrath*, Alexandros won't stand for it, Hades," Medusa stated in a matter-of-fact tone.

He set the picture down on his desk, and regarded her through veiled eyes. "You aren't going to tell him."

"What? Why not? He deserves to know. Callidora's life might be in danger!"

He shook his head with vehemence. "No, Edie, I forbid it."

She clamped her mouth closed with a loud report. He only spoke her nickname when he wanted her to fulfill whatever request he demanded. Apparently, this was one of those times.

"Don't call me that!" she balked, unable to meet his intense scrutiny.

"I must. You'll not do as I ask otherwise."

A fresh wave of tears rose to the surface. "What do you will of me?"

"I need time, Love."

"For?"

"To discover Artemis' plans. They obviously include your daughter. That much is apparent. I need to know what my niece is up to."

"Do you think she'll tell you?"

"Not really. Artemis always has her own agenda. What she wants, she gets. Hell, if Zeus weren't the king of Mount Olympus and ruler over the entire pantheon, she'd probably try to take the golden throne for herself."

Medusa's eyes widened with disbelief. "Surely, she wouldn't try such a thing, would she?"

"I wouldn't put it past her."

"I doubt that's what she's after, Hades. There must be something else. Something we're not seeing."

A swift knock upon the door of Hades' study cut off the rest of their conversation. He held up a hand and shook his head at Medusa. It was his signal that they'd finish their discussion later. She nodded with understanding. He settled back against his chair, and summoned the person forth. To their surprise, Persephone strode inside.

CHAPTER 2

Hades took note of the way Persephone's mouth tightened to a thin line as her emerald green eyes landed on Medusa. He was starting to suspect that his wife knew more about his relationship with the beautiful Gorgon than she let on. Granted, theirs was one of friendship, but it hadn't been like that at the beginning.

He'd taken Medusa under his wing decades ago, intent on keeping her safe and out of Athena's clutches. He hadn't approved of what his niece had done to Medusa in retaliation to Poseidon's defiling her temple when he'd raped the Gorgon within its walls. He'd also saved her from a certain death when Perseus had gone after her so that he could save Andromeda.

Though things weren't perfect between them, he was glad he'd saved Medusa's life. Her wit and charm endeared her to him all the more. There was nothing he wouldn't do to make sure that no harm came to her, much to his wife's chagrin. Shaking his head to clear it, he soon realized Persephone was speaking to him, sounding agitated.

"Come again?"

"I said I need your help with Cerberus. His lovely mate is ready to pop, and he won't let anyone near her. I'd like to be there when the pups are born, Hades. You promised that I could have one of my own."

He smiled and nodded, assessing his wife from head to toe. She wore a silk white peplos, her golden tresses pulled into a loose chignon. Several olive leaves adorned the base of her hairstyle, and a small gold tiara sat on top of her head. She'd wrapped a loose gold sash around her waist, and her feet were bare. She wasn't one for wearing shoes, as she liked the feel of the earth beneath her feet.

"Of course, Darling. Anything you wish."

She pouted and slid into the chair next to Medusa's. "Can we take care of things now?"

"In a few, yes. I was just having a word with Medusa."

"About?"

"Artemis."

"Oh? What has she done now?"

"What hasn't she done?" Hades quipped as he pushed himself to his feet, and strode over to the mini bar he'd installed to the right of the fireplace not too long ago. He poured himself a drink and downed it in one gulp. "The fool of a woman has taken a shining to Dora."

Persephone glanced at Medusa. "How so?"

"We're not sure," Medusa replied. "Hades just brought things to my attention."

"Our darling niece has decided that Medusa's daughter is one of Zeus' offspring."

Persephone snorted with amusement and rolled her eyes. "Oh, please. Zeus would never lay a hand on Medusa. No offense."

"None taken."

"He doesn't even know she's alive, for God's sake. Why would she even think such a thing?"

Hades grabbed the decanter of brandy and the crystal goblet he was drinking from, and took them with him back to his desk. He set them down and poured himself another drink. He offered the two women a drink, but they declined the gesture. Medusa wasn't a lover of hard liquor, and Persephone was in the beginning stages of motherhood, thus her refusal to imbibe.

"I asked Artemis as to what she could possibly want with a mortal. She claims she's curious about the girl and nothing more. I beg to differ. She's up to something."

"What could she want this time?" Persephone inquired.

Hades shrugged. "I'm not sure, but whatever it is, it revolves around Zeus."

Medusa shifted uncomfortably in her chair. "Should we mention things to Zeus?"

"No."

A slight frown marred the middle of Persephone's forehead. "Why not?"

"Like I said, I want to know what Artemis is up to. I want proof of her misdeeds before I bring Zeus into the fray."

"She's good at keeping secrets, husband."

Hades smiled broadly. "And I'm good at unlocking them. We'll know what she's up to soon enough."

"You really think it's that easy?" Medusa asked.

"Of course. I'll have to use your daughter as bait, though."

Medusa's glamour wore off at that given moment. She sat before him in her true form. The snakes sitting on top of her head hissed and snapped with agitation, her brown eyes blazing with anger. Her once pale skin was now covered with greenish-yellow scales. Slender hands were curled into vicious claws, ready to strike at a moment's notice. The lower half of her body had taken on the form of a snake, the rattle at the end of her tail twitching back and forth.

She often changed into her actual form whenever her anger got the best of her. Now was one of those times. He hated the fact that he'd brought her bad news, yet he knew she needed to know. Whatever Artemis planned for her daughter, it did not bode well. He wanted to prevent any unnecessary bloodshed.

Artemis might have found out about Callidora, but he was sure she didn't know who she truly was. He was aware of that fact that it was only a matter of time before she or someone else discovered that Medusa was very much alive. Zeus would not take kindly to his interference. He would cite that Athena had been in her right in dishing out the necessary punishment against Medusa. He'd probably make him turn the lovely Gorgon over to his niece when the time came. That, he could not allow.

"You'll do no ssssuch tttthing!" Medusa hissed as she pushed herself off the chair.

"I have to, Medusa. The girl intrigues Artemis to no end. By using her as leverage, we can discover what she's up to."

Her massive girth undulated back and forth as she shook her head. "No!"

"Hades is right. If Artemis plans deceit, we must discover it."

"Sssshe will hurt my baby!"

"I won't allow it. You have my word."

Medusa glared at him, refusing to hear anything more. She disappeared in the blink of an eye, leaving him to ponder the situation at hand. He needed her on his side if he was to succeed in protecting Callidora to the best of his ability. Somehow, some way, he'd bring her around to his way of thinking.

Persephone leaned forward and clasped his hand as it lay upon his desk. "I can talk to her for you, my Love."

"No," he said. "I'll take care of it. Shall we head on over to Cerberus' lair?"

She grinned and pushed herself to her feet. "Yes, please."

He stood and walked around his desk to pull his wife into his arms. "I love you. You know that, don't you?"

"Of course, and I love you, my dearest Hades."

She stood on the tips of her toes and pressed her lips against his. He accepted the kiss, and plundered her mouth with careless abandonment. For a moment, he was tempted to haul her back to his room and have his way with her, but there were far too many matters to take care. With one last look about the room, he orbed them to his favorite pet's lair, intent on fulfilling his wife's wishes.

CHAPTER 3

Hades dropped onto his favorite chair, and wiped the sweat off his brow. He and Persephone had spent the last several hours coaxing Grahdea, Cerberus' mate, into giving birth to her litter. Though the monster's name was not Greek, he loved it, nonetheless, as his wife had named the pup when he'd brought her home one day. Cerberus had taken a shining to the female, and kept to her side ever since.

Almost ten grueling hours later, they'd helped Grahdea deliver a five pup litter. The babies were just as vicious as their parents, yet he wouldn't have it any other way. Cerberus and his beloved mate guarded the gates to the Underworld, making sure that those who crossed the river, Styx, never escaped. The hellhounds were loyal to him, and did his bidding whenever possible.

Having selected the pup she'd raise once the hound was old enough, Hades had taken Persephone home and put her to bed. Though her pregnancy was still in the beginning stages, it was starting to take its toll on her. The morning sickness and the lethargic state she now found herself in bothered her the most. Motherhood suited her, however, as she was excited about the prospect of bearing him a son. Truth be told, he preferred that she give birth to a daughter, for he had a sneaking suspicion that she'd be the spitting image of her mother.

His eyes flew open as a loud grating pop resounded throughout the room. His niece, Athena, stood before him, her grey eyes angrily boring into him. He remained calm, a knowing smile spreading across his lips. Her eyes followed the motion, a muscle twitching across her jaw.

"You have something to tell me?" she prodded as she tapped her foot with impatience.

"In regards to?"

Her lips pursed together. "A secret, perhaps?"

He laughed and ran a hand through his thick dark brown curls. "A secret? Oh, I love these kinds of games! Tell me, whose secret should I be privy to?"

She growled and stamped her right foot against the wooden floor. "Damn it, Uncle. I have no time for humor. I'm serious. What have you been keeping from me?"

Hades settled back into the recliner, and crossed his arms about his chest. "Unless you hint as to what you're alluding to, I have no idea what the fuck you're talking about."

Athena waved her hands in the air, and produced a photograph. Hades' eyes widened as he watched the glossy paper float in his direction. He deftly caught it between his fingers.

Keeping his face impassive, he said, "What's this?"

"That, Uncle, is a picture of a painting I procured recently."

"Of?"

"Your consort."

"My consort?"

She nodded and flicked her golden hair over her right shoulder. "Yes. It has come to my attention that—"

Hades examined the picture once more. "This painting is of a woman who has long been dead, Athena. She no longer looks like this, either. You changed her remember? You gave her snakes for hair when you decided she was to pay for Poseidon's misdeeds."

Athena's chin rose with determination. "She enticed my uncle and defiled my temple. She paid the price for her duplicity."

Hades pushed himself to his feet and walked toward his desk, setting the photograph aside. Grabbing the crystal decanter full of brandy, he poured himself a glass and tossed it back. He soon poured himself another, hoping to delay the inevitable.

Somehow, Athena had gotten wind of the fact that Medusa was still alive. How that had come about, he did not know, but he intended to find out. Her life and that of her daughter's were in jeopardy, and he would not allow any harm to come to them. Not now. Not ever.

"Your wrath was unjust, Athena. Poseidon raped her in your temple as a means of lashing out at you."

"That was never proven."

"It was. You refused to see reason, that's all," he replied as he downed another glass.

She sighed with exasperation and shook her head in denial. "Poseidon would never do such a thing."

He slammed the empty goblet down upon his desk and turned to face her. "You have no idea what Poseidon is capable of."

Her mouth thinned to a tight line. "He wouldn't sully his hands by taking a woman's honor."

"How would you know? We've all done things we're not proud of Athena. Poseidon made a decision that changed several lives. It's a mistake he can't undo, unfortunately. You, on the other hand, could have admitted defeat. Medusa's livelihood was in question, yet you chose to remain firm in the belief that she was at fault for Poseidon's actions."

"She was!"

"She was not, and you know it. Because of your misplaced beliefs, a woman paid the price for something she didn't do."

Athena snorted with derision. "But she's not dead, is she?"

Hades maintained his haughty facade and said, "Yes, she is."

"I beg to differ."

"Do you?"

"Yes. I have proof."

He pointed to the photograph. "That is hardly proof."

She laughed and rolled her eyes at him. "No, Uncle,

not that. Someone has seen Medusa with their very eyes. He would never lie to me."

"Are you sure?"

She grinned. "Of course. My source and I are thick as thieves."

He tilted his head at her in contemplation. "I see. Who is this *source*? Why keep him a secret?"

Her smile wavered. Panic spread through the depths of her eyes.

"I'm not."

"Then tell me who he is."

A harried Hermes materialized before Athena had a chance of saying more. "Athena . . ." he stammered as he tried to catch his breath. "I . . . I have news.

Hades' eyes narrowed as he stared at his nephew. "Do tell."

Hermes swung around to face him. His blue eyes widened with surprise. Hades watched as his porcelain features paled beneath the onslaught of his angry gaze. For the first time in his life, he saw his nephew do something unexpected. He fainted.

CHAPTER 4

Hades smirked with amusement as Hermes came to. His nephew stared up at the pair with slight scowl on his face. Taking a deep breath, he bent forward and grabbed Hermes' hands, pulling him to his feet. The younger god dusted off his jeans, his face flushed with embarrassment.

"Sorry. I've never done that sort of thing before."

"Could have fooled me," Hades replied.

Athena sighed with exasperation. "Is there something you want?"

"Yes."

"And?"

"I need to talk to you."

"About?"

Hermes clenched his teeth together, a muscle twitching along his lower jaw. "Something."

Hades cleared his throat, drawing their attention to him. "It sounds as if whatever Hermes has to say is personal, so I suggest you take your debate elsewhere,

Athena. I've matters I need to attend to."

Her grey eyes were alight with anger. "What could possibly be more important than what we were discussing, Uncle?" she stated bluntly.

He dropped his six-foot-two frame onto the chair behind his desk, running a hand through his hair once more. "A good many things," he quipped. "Whatever arguments you have are invalid. Medusa is dead. Let's leave it at that."

"No, she's not," Hermes interjected.

Hades' eyes narrowed as his gaze fell upon his nephew. "Come again?"

Hermes' face became infused with a deep magenta color as he engaged in a silent battle of wills with him. "She's not. I've seen her with my very eyes!"

The hairs on the back of Hades' neck stood on end as he became cognizant of who Athena's unknown source was. "Have you?"

"Yes."

"Where?"

His nephew pulled himself up to his full height of five-feet-eleven. A triumphant smile spread across his face.

"Here."

"Here?"

"Yes. Not too long ago, in fact."

Hades slammed his right fist against the desk's surface. His nostrils flared outward as he tried to control his rising anger.

"You've been walking around in my palace without

my knowing?"

Hermes' features blanched. "I was coming to see you!"

"Why didn't you announce yourself?"

"I didn't see the need."

Hades' face purpled with fury. "You saw no need?"

"No. I'm—"

He cut Hermes off abruptly. "You're what? Just because you're family doesn't mean you can trounce about unannounced. This is my home. Therefore, you abide by MY rules. Is that understood?"

"But . . ." Hermes' resolve crumbled beneath his dark, turbulent gaze. "Fine."

"Now, get out."

"I'm not done yet."

"You are now. I've heard enough."

He watched as his nephew turned to face Athena, holding his hands out in supplication. Athena shook her head and promptly dropped her gaze to the floor. Hermes' shoulders slumped with defeat. With one last glance in Hades' direction, he disappeared.

He assessed his niece from head to toe, trying to make sense of the situation at hand. The fact that Hermes was now privy to Medusa's existence bothered him. He'd been so careful, yet his efforts weren't enough, apparently. While he might be able to claim that what Hermes had seen was a figment of his imagination, given his extremely frivolous ways, the damage had been done.

His nephew's claims had incited Athena's curiosity, and she would not rest until she had the necessary proof that Medusa was, in fact, alive within her very hands. He didn't doubt, for a second, that she'd find what she was looking for. The question was, how would he be able to delay her from breaking open a massive can of worms in the process?

Zeus would have his head because of his deception. He'd stepped into the line of fire from the moment he'd decided to save Medusa's life. Yet he couldn't keep himself from doing so. Medusa hadn't deserved the pain and heartache Athena had subjected her to. He would bear the brunt of Zeus' wrath if it meant that no harm would come to Medusa and her beloved offspring.

The sound of Athena clearing her throat brought him back to the present. He sat up straight, rubbing his hands across his flushed cheeks. The weight of what he now needed to do sat heavily upon his shoulders. He prayed that his efforts wouldn't be for naught when the time came.

"Yes?"

"We haven't finished our discussion," she murmured offhandedly.

He pushed himself to his feet, glaring in her direction. "As far as I'm concerned, Athena, yes, we have."

She crossed her arms upon her chest once more. "You're hiding something. I'm sure of it."

He snorted and shook his head. "Let me guess. You're going to try to discover my secrets."

"Yes."

He laughed. "Discover away."

"This is no time for such amusements, Uncle. I'm being serious here."

"I know. That's what amuses me."

Her eyes narrowed, her mouth pressed to a tight line. "You will pay for your deceit if it comes to light that Medusa still lives."

His mirth dissipated, and he stared at her with distaste. "I'm not the one who will pay for such mistakes."

"So you admit it?"

"Admit what?"

"That's she's still alive."

"No, Athena, I do not. I am only making light of past occurrences. We've both done things we're not proud of. You would do well to remember that."

She frowned. "How is this pertinent to all things Medusa?"

"It is, and it isn't."

"What does that mean?"

"You figure it out," he replied, and waved a hand in front of him, promptly transporting her back to Mount Olympus without another word.

CHAPTER 5

Hades pushed himself to his feet, running an unsteady hand through his hair. An impatient sigh slid past his lips as he strode to the door. He could have teleported himself to his chambers, but he had no desire in disrupting Persephone's rest in doing so. Instead, he'd take his time in getting there. The walk to his bedroom would allow him to clear his head.

Closing the door behind him, he trudged down the semi-darkened hallway. His thoughts centered on Medusa and the secrets they shared. The thought of Zeus exacting his retribution once he learned of her continued existence did not sit well with him. He'd made the decision to preserve her life in the hopes that he'd be able to get Athena to reverse what she'd done to the girl. He knew now, that she would never do so. She'd made that fact abundantly clear not too long ago.

Most of the gods and goddesses considered him to be cold and callous, something he was clearly not. He supposed they saw him in this manner because he ruled the Underworld, making sure that the dead were taken to their proper places. In a sense, the idea of being a careless tyrant did suit him, but that was not an active role he pursued.

He loved and cared for those he took under his wing. Yes, he depicted himself as something he was not, but that was only for appearances sake. Doing so gave him the necessary freedom to protect his loved ones without anyone being none-the-wiser as to who or what he loved the most. Now, unfortunately, his livelihood was being threatened. Granted, Athena and Hermes were only working on assumptions. They had no idea that Medusa was truly alive.

He might have been able to claim that Hermes was well into his cups if it came down to it, but he knew better. Sooner or later, everyone on Mount Olympus would know that the Gorgon still lived. He would be able to minimize the backlash from his having kept her hidden for so long, but it would not erase the fact that he'd gone against Zeus' wishes. She should have died by Perseus' hands back then. Her legacy should not have continued. Yet he knew he could not let her perish in such a manner. He'd gladly do the same things again if it ever came to that.

His heart raced inside his chest as he came to a stop in front of the door leading to his personal quarters. The thought of what he needed to do ate at him. He didn't want to cause Persephone any further pain. Most especially now that she was pregnant with his child. Yet he needed to set things straight. It was the only way he could proceed with the next part of his plan.

Taking a deep breath, he pushed the door open and strode inside. His heart swelled with pride as he stared at a sleeping Persephone as she lay on his bed. Her arms were wrapped around a full-length body pillow, her golden hair spread across her bare shoulders in every direction. Her long, dark lashes fluttered as she dreamt, soft snores sliding past her lips.

He grew hard as her body twitched as she slept, the bedsheet slipping downward to expose her engorged breasts. The thought of slipping into bed and taking her while she slept appealed to him. He'd pull the sheet lower until her sex was completely exposed. Utilizing his lips and tongue, he'd bring her to climax, time and again, before he'd sate himself within her, once and for all.

Persephone stirred in her sleep, his name spilling off her tongue as she rolled onto her back. "Hades?"

"Y–Yes?" he breathed, trying to pull himself together.

"Where were you?" she asked sleepily, her emerald green fluttering open.

"In my study."

She stifled a yawn and stretched her tired limbs. "You work too much."

He tugged off his shirt and tossed it aside, striding in her direction. "I have to. I'm the Lord of the Underworld."

"Even gods need a break, too," she proclaimed.

He unbuckled and unzipped his pants, pushing them

down his hips. He kicked the denim fabric aside before sliding into the bed.

"I take far too many as it is, Love," he murmured as he spooned himself against her.

"One more won't kill you."

He nuzzled the warm hollow of her shoulder, gently nipping at her flesh. "I suppose not."

She turned around to face him, pressing her mouth against his. "I know so!"

He lost himself to the kiss, allowing his hands to roam his wife's body at will. Persephone responded to his touch, giving him as much as he took. He gave in to the pleasure, enjoying what his wife had to offer.

Tomorrow was another day, he surmised. Mount Olympus, Medusa, and the world's troubles could wait until then. Tonight, he belonged to Persephone. Her wish was his command, and he would have it no other way.

CHAPTER 6

Hades awoke to find himself alone in his bed.
Persephone was nowhere to be found. The only sign that
she'd been in the room with him in the first place was the
imprint of her head embedded into the pillow nearby.

A wave of trepidation filled him as a slew of
possibilities of where she could be coursed through his
head. He told himself that nothing was amiss. That she
was probably in the bathroom nearby. His fears were
confirmed, however, when he rolled onto his side and
something crinkled beneath him. He shoved the
bedsheets aside to find the Post-It note his wife had left
him penned in her elegant handwriting.

Mother has summoned me, it said. *I shan't be gone long, my
dear. Please, don't fret. I'm as safe as I can be in Mother's hands. I
promise! Love you!*

He blinked rapidly to keep his tears at bay. She'd
taken the time to reassure him before leaving to attend to
her mother's wishes. The gesture alone spoke volumes.

He brought the piece of paper to his nose, inhaling the scent of her perfume that she'd sprayed upon it. That, too, made him miss her all the more.

He reached out to put the paper down on the night stand before sliding out of bed. Striding in the bathroom's direction, he quickly hopped in the shower, and rinsed the evidence of the night's activities from his skin. Feeling refreshed, he hurried about and pulled on a pair of black jeans, a white t-shirt, a pair of expensive black combat boots, and his favorite pair of Ray Bans sunglasses. He ran a comb through his hair, and smiled as he gazed at his reflection in the mirror.

Satisfied with his appearance, he grabbed his keys and hurried out of his bedroom. Walking through the halls, he headed toward Cerberus' enclosure, and gave his pet a bite to eat. He set enough out for Grahdea as well. Once that was done, he headed toward his office to pick up his favorite sword.

With several quick flicks of his hands, he'd reduced the sword to the size of a Swiss Army knife. He pocketed the blade and nodded with satisfaction. There was quite a bit he needed to take care of today. Loose ends he hoped to tighten up, once and for all.

First on his list was a chat with Medusa. Things hadn't ended well with her yesterday, and he needed to fix everything, pronto. He prayed that she'd forgive him for what he planned to do.

If he was to succeed in beating Artemis at her own game, he needed to stoop to her own level. Doing so meant that he'd end up doing things he didn't want to do.

Yet if it ensured that his loved ones would be safe in the long run, perhaps his duplicity would be worth the pain and heartache that was soon to follow.

CHAPTER 7

Hades materialized in the middle of Medusa's bathroom, smiling broadly as she scrambled to stand up in the middle of her hot tub. Her blue eyes blazed with anger, and her chin lifted with defiance. His dark eyes roved up and down the entire length of her body, watching as the soapy suds slid down her flesh. Against his will, his body tightened with wanting.

"What are you doing here?" she hissed, curling her arms across her chest.

"We need to talk."

"You could have called!"

"That would have defeated my purpose in catching up with you. You'd have done everything to avoid me."

She glared at him. "We have nothing to talk about."

"Don't we?"

"No."

"Now, Edie . . ."

"Don't even go there!" she growled as she stepped

out of the tub and grabbed the towel hanging nearby. "I hate it when you do that!"

He smirked with amusement. "That's only because you seem to listen when I call you by your nickname."

"Of course, I do!"

His smile disappeared as he took a step toward her. "We really do need to talk."

She strode past him into the adjoining bedroom, her teeth clenched tight as she fought to keep a tight rein on her emotions. "What is it that you want, Hades?"

He followed her into the room, watching as she reached for a thin black negligee lying on top of the bed. The towel pooled at her feet as she let go of it. For a moment, he allowed himself to enjoy the sight of her plump derriere exposed to his view. His cock hardened painfully as she bent over to the pick up the discarded towel. Her well-shaved pussy was momentarily visible.

She straightened, tossing the towel upon the bed, before tugging the negligee over her head. A knowing smile played about her lips. Medusa knew how to push his buttons and wasn't afraid to use his attraction for her to her advantage.

He held his breath as she hopped onto the bed, and turned around to face him. She laid back, her black silky hair spreading across her pillow. Spreading her legs wide, her left hand dove between her legs. He followed the motion with his eyes, and watched as she opened her pink lips with several of her fingers. The sight of her doing so played havoc on his libido.

"Edie . . ."

Medusa grinned. "Yes?"

"You're killing me here!"

Her legs scissored close as she stared back at him. "It's nice to know that I can still affect you."

He growled with frustration. "There was never any question of that."

She sat up, scowling deeply at him. "Does Persephone know?"

"About?"

"Us."

"No."

Her eyes widened at the admission. "Why not?"

He shrugged. "I've seen no need to inform her of our past."

"She should know, Hades."

"Should she?"

"I think so. It's only fair."

He sighed and strode in her direction. "In time," he said, taking a seat on the edge of her bed.

She moved toward him and wrapped her arms around his neck. "I sort of understand why you're keeping me a secret, but you don't have to."

"Don't I?"

She nuzzled the side of his neck, gently nipping at his flesh. "No."

He reached up to clasp her left hand in his. "You know I do, Edie."

"No, you don't."

He pulled her around so that she sat across his lap. He did his best to ignore the incessant throb of his cock as she settled herself against him.

"I do. Callidora's future is at stake. You know that as well as I do."

"Why?" she asked. "Because Artemis now knows of her?"

"Yes."

"Your niece doesn't know about her true parentage. No one does, aside from you, me, and Alexandros. Alex would never say a word. He loves Callidora dearly."

He stared down into her blue eyes. "I know, but there are ways for people to get a hold of the necessary information. Artemis—"

"Artemis, what? She doesn't know anything, and she never will," Medusa replied as she pushed herself off of Hades' lap.

He crossed his arms about his chest. "Won't she?"

"No."

"She thinks Zeus sired her, Edie."

Medusa whirled around to face him. "Why would she think such a thing?"

"I don't know."

"Surely, she must have said something to clarify that claim?"

"Not really. That's what I tried to tell you the other night before you succinctly disappeared on me. I'm not sure as to what Artemis wants, but I have a feeling Callidora fits into her plans somehow. She's fixated on the girl. More so, than she's ever been with anyone in the past."

"Then get her to turn her attention elsewhere."

"I'm trying."

"Then try harder!" she cried, her blue eyes filling with tears.

Hades sprung off the bed and pulled her into his arms. "I am," he said as he buried his face within the fragrant curls of her hair.

Medusa clung to him, her shoulders shaking as she gave in to the pain radiating within her. He knew she feared for her daughter. Keeping Callidora's existence a secret had been essential to her survival. It had kept Zeus and Athena from discovering that Medusa was alive. Now, her very world was being threatened by his niece's curiosity. He knew he needed to nip that curiosity in the bud. The question was, how could he keep Medusa and her daughter free of harm, and still do what he needed to do in the process?

CHAPTER 8

The sound of someone clearing their throat drew Hades' attention. He carefully disengaged himself from Medusa's embrace as his turbulent gaze swung to the open doorway of her bedroom. Alexandros stood within it, casually leaning against the doorjamb. His blue eyes narrowed to half slits as he surveyed the scene. Medusa turned toward him, wiping the backs of her hands across her cheeks.

"You're home!"

A muscle twitched along the god's jaw. "Yes. I have been for quite some time now."

"You have?"

Alexandros nodded. "Yes. I caught part of your little display just now. I'm amazed by your self-control, Hades. I'd have pounded that pussy by now," he quipped.

Hades bit down on the inside corner of his lip to keep himself from grinning. The last thing he wanted to do was piss off the *God of Wrath*.

"Yes, well, it's sometimes not that hard to resist a

beautiful woman."

Alexandros pushed himself into the room, and made his way toward Medusa. He clasped her left arm tight, and dragged her over to her bed. He promptly picked her up and unceremoniously dumped her in the middle of the bed. The bed's springs creaked beneath the onslaught of the sudden weight.

Hades watched as the *God of Wrath* wrapped his hands around Medusa's ankles and bound them to the bed. He then hurried around to the other side of the bed, securing her wrists to the headboard. Medusa struggled against her bindings, her breath catching as she stared into her lover's eyes.

"Shall I leave you both alone?"

Alexandros turned to face him. His eyes darkened as he smiled.

"No."

"Are you sure?"

His cousin pointed to the beautiful temptress lying on the bed. "She obviously interests you, and from what I can see, you want her just as much as I do."

Hades' eyes swung toward the bed. "She's beautiful, yes, but I didn't come here for a quick fuck."

"No?"

"No."

Suspicion clouded Alexandros' eyes. "Then what did you come here for?"

"How much of the conversation did you catch?"

Blood rushed toward Alexandros' face, painting it red. "Not much, actually. I was focused on what Tasha was doing, in all honesty."

"Medusa!"

Alexandros smirked as he turned to face her. "Tasha! You know as well as I do that we must keep up appearances. If those on Mount Olympus are to continue believing that you are dead, then we mustn't call you by your true name. Therefore, I—"

"Yeah, about that . . ." Hades murmured. "Her safety and that of Callidora might have been compromised."

"What!?" Alexandros sputtered as he turned around to face Hades. "How the fuck did that happen?"

Hades shifted uncomfortably from foot to foot. "Hermes came upon us a couple days ago. He saw Medusa turn, and took word of it to Athena. I—"

"Athena? Athena now knows she's alive?"

"Well, no, not exactly."

Alexandros swore with vehemence and began to pace the entire length of the room. Hades and Medusa looked on as he spoke to himself beneath his breath. Their gazes clashed. The angst and pain in her eyes tugged upon Hades' heartstrings. He hated hurting her, and wished he could avoid doing so. Yet the situation was out of his hands until he could bring things back under control.

"You're going to take care of things, are you not?" Alexandros inquired, moments later, as he dropped his six-foot-seven frame onto the recliner sitting in front of the fireplace.

"Yes. Working on things, as we speak. I should—"

"Then get to it. If anything happens to MY daughter,

I'm coming after you, Hades. And I don't give a fuck about the fact that you're the *Lord of the Underworld.*"

Medusa gasped with surprise. "Alex!"

"'Tis true, darling, I don't. All that matters to me is that my family is safe. Hades promised that no one would know of your existence. That promise has been broken. 'Tis time to pay up."

A muscle twitched along Hades' jaw. "I'm doing the best I can, Alex. I'll sort things out. Trust me on that. In the meantime, do everything possible to keep Callidora and her mother safe. Athena isn't the only one who's aware of them. Artemis is skulking in the corners, too."

With that said, Hades orbed himself out of Medusa's quarters before Alexandros had a chance of uttering a reply. He materialized in the middle of the sidewalk on Sixth Avenue, moments later. People pushed past him as they sought to get to where they were going, oblivious to the fact that he hadn't been standing there not too long ago.

CHAPTER 9

Hades willed himself into an invisible state as a slender redhead standing nearby caught his attention. He leaned against the nearest light post, smirking with amusement as he watched Artemis press her face against the glass of the store she was looking into. Her auburn hair fluttered gently as a slight breeze began to pick up.

He wasn't pleased about the fact that his niece now knew of Medusa's daughter. He'd thought the girl was a well-kept secret, one no one would have known about. Yet he'd been mistaken on that part. The fact that Callidora was now tied to the prophecy concerning the *Child of Calamity* did not sit well with him. Though, he knew there was nothing he could do to change the events that were now unfolding before his very eyes.

His eyes narrowed as his gaze fell upon a mannequin in the window. A silk blue dress adorned the plastic body, the folds of its a-line skirt barely reaching the mannequin's knees. An idea unfolded in his mind as he eyed both his niece and the mannequin nearby. She obviously needed to get the sight of Callidora out of her system, and this was the perfect opportunity for her to do just that.

Waving his hands in the air in front of him, Hades changed the composition of the dress. A silvery-yellow strapless dress now adorned the mannequin. Gold and green leaves spread across the bodice's border, inching toward its seam, and down to its hem. Interspersed with the leaves were images of a huntress holding a bow and arrow as numerous animals crowded around her. The ivy flared upward and came to a stop at the V-shape holding the bodice and flared skirt together.

Satisfied with his creation, he gently pushed his power in Artemis' direction, and carefully drew her attention to the dress in the window. Her eyes widened as she witnessed the dress's final transformation take place. Hades' body solidified as he came to stand beside her. She turned to face him, a look of surprise etched across her beautiful face.

"Hades!" she gasped. "What are you doing here?"

He shrugged nonchalantly. "Window shopping, and you?"

Her cheeks flushed with color. "The same, I suppose."

His gaze swung toward the dress. "Beautiful, isn't it?"

"What?"

"The dress."

She turned around to stare at it once more, admiring

the garment's beauty. "Yes, it is. You made it, didn't you?"

He grinned at her. "Of course. Go on in. Try it on."

"But . . ."

"You know you want to, so I'm giving you the opportunity you seek. Consider this a gift, though it comes with a warning."

"Yes?"

"The girl must not come to harm. None. At all. Is that understood?"

She frowned. "How did you . . . ?"

His eyes gleamed with suppressed menace. "I have my ways. You're not the only one searching for answers, Artemis."

"Hades . . ."

"You must hurry. Time is of the essence, so make use of it!" Without another word, he teleported himself back home.

CHAPTER 10

A startled cry was rent from Hades' lips as he landed in the middle of his study. Persephone sat in his favorite chair, her legs draped across its left armrest. Her dainty ankles were crossed together, her right foot tapping the air with impatience. Her emerald green gaze was trained on his face, her mouth thinned to a tight line.

"Persephone!" he said, dropping his tall frame onto the chair in front of his desk. "What are you doing here? I thought you were at your mother's place."

She nonchalantly examined the fingernails of her left hand before turning her attention back to him. "I was."

"But . . . ?"

"I was inadvertently summoned elsewhere."

He raised a brow in question. "Oh?"

She dropped her feet to the floor, and made herself comfortable in Hades' favorite chair. "Is there something you want to tell me?"

"Such as?"

She shrugged, refusing to be lenient with him. "I don't know, Dearest. Why don't you tell me?"

He released a sigh of frustration as he crossed his arms upon his chest. "Persephone . . ."

A muscle twitched along her lower jaw as she stared back at him. "You've been keeping secrets, Hades."

The hairs on the back of his neck rose with apprehension. He feared what she had to say, then and there. *There's no way she could know about Edie and me. I've been far too careful!*

As if she'd read his thoughts, Persephone replied, "I know about your affair with Medusa."

His tanned features blanched. "Honey, I . . ."

"We were married!"

"We still are," he inserted smoothly.

She glared at him. "That's beside the point."

"Persephone, I—"

She lifted a hand to silence him. "How recent was it?"

He sighed and ran a hand through his thick, dark curls. "It was a long time ago."

"When?"

"Honey . . ."

She leaned forward to bang her right fist across the surface of his desk. "When, Hades?"

His dark eyes bored into hers as he tried to assess the situation. He wasn't used to seeing her so angry. Not since he'd kidnapped her so long ago. He'd chalk down her irritation to the fact that she was pregnant, but he knew that wasn't the cause of her distress. He was, however unwittingly that fact came about.

He released a pent-up breath and shifted uncomfortably in his chair. "My affair came about several weeks after I rescued her from what would have been her untimely demise."

His heart hammered within his chest as he thought about his excursion with Medusa centuries ago. Persephone would have skewered him by the balls the moment she'd found out about it. She'd bust his kneecaps, too, once she found out about the fact that the two of them shared more than just a random night or two between them.

"It's been centuries!?"

"More or less. Time is irrelevant, however. For the gods, anyway."

She sat up straight, a slight frown marring her forehead. "Do you love her?" she prodded, her voice barely a whisper.

"Persephone . . ."

His gentle tone annoyed her. "DO YOU LOVE HER!?"

"Not like I love you," he admitted.

She glanced down at her hands as they lay on her lap. Though he could not see her face, he was sure she was crying. He hated the fact that he was hurting her. He'd thought his affair with Medusa was a thing of the past, something he'd never have to admit to. Yet he'd been wrong on that account.

Still, he wouldn't change the way things had come about. Medusa had given him the one thing he treasured the most. He'd do everything in his power to protect that beautiful blessing. Someone obviously wanted to wreak havoc on his life. Whoever it was wanted the truth known, though he wasn't quite sure as to why.

Unless . . .

The sound of Persephone clearing her throat broke through his turbulent thoughts. He looked up to find her murderous glare trained on his face. He'd inadvertently missed something important.

"I'm sorry, what?"

She frowned and shook her head at him in dismay. "I hate it when you do that."

His face flushed with embarrassment. "I didn't mean to."

She pushed herself to her feet and walked around the desk to sit on the upper right corner of it. Hades' cock twitched with anticipation as he eyed the silky smooth golden skin of her upper thigh as it peeked through the side slit of her black ankle-length skirt. His left cheek smarted as she slapped her hand across his flesh.

"Damn it, Hades, stop that!"

He stared into her eyes, aching to lose himself in their green glittery depths. Persephone meant everything to him. If he were to lose her now . . .

"Forgive me, Love, it's just . . ."

"You can't keep your cock in your pants, I know."

"What? No! That's not—"

"Oh, please," she breathed, deftly cutting off his retort. "You just admitted to an affair. Surely, that cinches that statement, fair and square?"

His shoulders slumped with defeat. "I guess."

"I don't presume to know why you've done what you've done, Hades, but there will be no more of it."

"I haven't–"

She ignored him and continued with her tirade. "I don't care. I don't want to hear it, either. It's over and done with. Is that understood?"

He shifted uncomfortably in his chair. "Yes."

She nodded, a stoic expression flitting across her face. "There's just one last thing I need to know."

"Sure."

She stood up once more and dug her hand into the right pocket of her skirt. Hades' pulse raced as he spied the edge of a photograph he'd seem one too many times. Persephone smoothed the crinkled glossy paper, and regarded it intently for a moment or two before she presented it to him. With a trembling hand, he accepted the picture, and stared down at a face he knew as well as his own.

"Is she yours?"

"Persephone, I–"

"IS SHE YOURS?"

He sighed and said, "Yes."

Her eyes bored into his as she stared down at him. Her mouth thinned to an even tighter line as a bright sheen of moisture shone in her eyes. He pushed himself to his feet, intent on comforting her. Yet he never got the chance to. Persephone disappeared in the blink of an eye, leaving him to ponder whether they'd weather yet another storm, this time one of his own making.

CHAPTER 11

Blinking rapidly to combat the tears rising to the surface, Hades slammed his fist down across the desk's edge in frustration. He no longer doubted that someone was out to destroy him and the pantheon. Someone obviously knew more than they let on. Whoever it was wanted him to know that fact.

But who could it be? he wondered. *Why would they want to destroy me? What purpose would it serve?*

Before he had the chance to ponder more of his predicament, he felt Zeus' pull as his brother summoned him to Mount Olympus. He growled with annoyance, and teleported himself to his brother's private quarters. He found Zeus bent over a table, pouring over several scrolls.

"What?" he barked as he strode over to him, and grabbed the pitcher of wine sitting nearby. He poured himself a glass with a quick flick of his hand.

Zeus straightened and assessed him from head to

toe. "Women troubles?" he quipped lightly.

"Somewhat."

"Want to talk about it?"

Hades fixed a scathing look upon his older brother. "No."

"I'm all ears, brother."

"I said, no. Since when do I confide in you, anyway?"

Zeus placed a hand on his left shoulder. "We all need confidants somewhere along the line. Consider me yours."

He dropped onto the nearest chair and pulled the scroll Zeus had been perusing moments ago to him. "What did you summon me here for?"

"I'm in a bit of a dilemma."

"Oh?"

Pulling out another chair, Zeus sat down and pointed to the scroll in front of him. "Do you know what 'at scroll hides within its folds?"

Hades fingered the edge of the parchment and nodded. "Yes."

"And?"

"It's the prophecy about the *Child of Calamity*."

"Aye."

"What about it?"

"Do you believe in it?"

"Zeus . . ."

"Humor me, brother. Please."

"Fine."

"I ask again, do you believe in it?"

Hades bit down on the right corner of lower lip in

thought. *Do I believe in the prophecy?* he wondered. There were a good many that did, but was he one of them?

Artemis believed that his daughter, Callidora, was the one the prophecy spoke of. So much so, that she was hell-bent on wreaking havoc on Mount Olympus because of her beliefs. He'd heard of the prophecy for as long as he could remember. This entire time he'd thought one of Zeus' offspring would bring forth the supposed apocalypse.

Is it possible we've been wrong on that account? Could it be that my having meddled in Medusa's affairs changed things as we know it? If so, what will become of me—of us?

Zeus tapped him across the shoulder, drawing his attention back to the matter at hand. "Well?"

"I'm not sure."

"You've known about the prophecy for centuries, Hades. Either you believe in it, or you don't."

He stood up and began to pace across the length of Zeus' study. His mind raced with the implications of his past actions. His brother had no idea that Medusa was still alive, a fact he wanted to keep hidden for as long as possible. There was no telling what Zeus would do were he to know that Hades had thwarted his plans so long ago.

"I don't," he said. "At least, I didn't."

Zeus frowned. "So you do?"

"No."

"I don't understand."

"That prophecy speaks of a child that can ultimately destroy the world and the pantheon itself. Do you honestly believe such a being exists?"

"I do now."

"How so?"

"There have been rumors spoken amongst our brethren. Some say the child has been born."

"Have you seen it?"

"No."

"Then how do you know the child exists?"

"I've heard—"

"Rumors, I know. Have you considered that what our people have spoken about could be just that— rumors?"

Zeus bristled with indignation. "How could it be? The prophecy clearly—"

"THAT prophecy was a lie."

Zeus' face paled beneath the onslaught of his words. "You know?" he whispered.

Hades came to stand beside the panoramic window, his back turned to Zeus. "Yes."

"For how long?"

A soft sigh escaped Hades' lips. "From the moment you and Hera sat down to create it."

"But . . ."

He turned around to face his older brother. "I was looking for you that day. A source told me you went to see Hera, so I made my way to her estate. I arrived in the nick of time to hear the two of you plot about the prophecy itself."

Several lines of stress broke out around the corners of Zeus' mouth. "You never said . . ."

"Why would I? The prophecy was a convenience at the time."

"And now?"

"It's a fucking hindrance."

"I'll have you know—"

"Save it. I don't want to hear it. You're in a bind. I get that. I suppose you want me to look into the matter?"

"Well, no."

"Then what?"

Zeus shifted in his chair to pull another scroll to him. He unfurled the parchment and carefully spread it across the table. The prophecy itself was scratched into the vellum's center. Below that lay a graph depicting the main gods and goddesses of the pantheon. The names of several lesser gods and goddesses were also jotted down in the margins.

The significance of the scroll was quite clear. His brother suspected several of the gods and goddesses of treachery. Though he wasn't sure as to who could have set things into motion, someone out there knew more than they were saying. Without so much as saying the words, Hades understood what Zeus wanted from him.

In his mind, he held him clear of any association with everything that had to do with the *Child of Calamity*. That made him the perfect scapegoat to dig a little deeper into the situation at hand. No one would suspect him of being in cahoots with Zeus. It was well-known within the pantheon that the two of them didn't get along that well.

Yet here I am, waiting to do my brother's bidding. How fucking ironic!

Without uttering a single word, Hades grabbed the scroll and quickly re-rolled it. He sealed its edge closed and shrank the roll so that it would fit in the confines of his pocket. Stowing it within its depths, he stared deep into Zeus' eyes.

"I'll be in touch," he said, and promptly disappeared.

CHAPTER 12

The hairs on the back of Hades' neck rose as he dropped the scroll Zeus gave him into his private vault. He swung the safe's door closed and turned around to reprimand the intruder only to find Persephone standing in front of him. She was immaculately dressed a blue pinstripe suit with a white silk blouse underneath its jacket. Her dainty feet were encased in a pair of three inch Jimmy Choo heels, adding to her impressive height of five-feet-ten.

His lower body tightened with wanting as his eyes roved over her body. The euphoria was short-lived, however, as his gaze fell upon the suitcase sitting next to her right foot. His mouth grew dry as realization dawned on him. She was leaving, and she wanted him to know it.

"I'm going to stay with my mother for a few days," she said softly.

"What? Why?"

She released the breath she'd been holding, and

slipped her hands into her pant's pockets. "I need some time alone."

"For what?"

"To think things over."

He moved toward her, intent on pulling her into his arms, but she smoothly stepped to the side. "What is there to think about?" he asked, refusing to accept the fact that she was leaving him.

"You lied to me."

"I didn't mean to."

"Bullshit, Hades. You did. You're the master of secrets. God knows what else you're keeping from me."

"I'm not—"

"I'm pretty sure you are. How long was it going take before you confided in me?"

A wave of color spread across Hades' face. "I wanted to. I just . . ."

"You couldn't," she supplied, her voice full of bitterness.

"Yes."

"Let me guess. It's because you feel quite guilty."

"No. Well, yes!" he said a tad too quickly.

A look of dismay flitted across her face before she gathered her composure, and pretended that he hadn't said a word. "I'm going to be gone awhile."

"You can't be. We have an agreement. The seasons . . ."

She pinned her heated gaze upon him, refusing to allow herself to feel a bit of warmth toward him. "The seasons will get on just fine without me. Winter has begun, and it'll continue on its merry path."

"I need you here to control it."

"No, you don't."

"Persephone . . ."

"I need some time away from you, Hades. To sort things out inside my head."

"But . . ."

"Please."

Pain coursed through him as he realized that he had no other option but to let her go. If they were going to salvage their relationship somehow, he needed to show her that he trusted her. Even if it meant letting her go in order to do so.

"Very well."

A sigh of relief escaped her. She took a step toward him, intent on giving him a quick kiss, but she caught herself at the last minute. Instead, she raised a hand at him and waved goodbye before teleporting herself and her luggage to her mother's house.

He stared at the spot she'd been standing in, moments ago, unwilling to accept that she was gone. He told himself that she'd come back. That they'd overcome this storm as well. Yet he knew better. There was no telling as to how things would turn out between them. He'd inadvertently dealt her a smarting blow, one he wasn't sure she'd ever recover from.

CHAPTER 13

"A penny for your thoughts," Poseidon murmured as he sat down on the bar stool next to Hades.

Hades glared at his brother before knocking back a shot of whiskey. He'd made his way to the Hard Rock Café with the intention of drowning his sorrows in several bottles of liquor. He'd chosen a place out of the way, one that would afford him the privacy he yearned for. Never once, had he expected to see anyone from the pantheon show up, much less Poseidon.

"What do you want?"

Poseidon smirked and said, "You're a hard man to track down. I never thought I'd find you in a place like this. Though, I do think the Hard Rock Cafe's atmosphere does suit you."

Hades snorted with derision and rolled his eyes. "I'm not in the mood for whatever you have in mind."

"What makes you think I have anything on my mind?"

His dark eyes bored into Poseidon's. "You're here for a reason."

Poseidon's sure smile faltered. "You know me so well."

"I should. You're my brother."

Digging into his pockets, Poseidon withdrew a piece of paper, and set it down on the counter in front of Hades. He stared resolutely at the photograph, the lines around his mouth tightening with displeasure. As much as he loved his daughter, he was getting tired of seeing her picture everywhere he went. How his brother had gotten a hold of a copy of it, he did not know, but he was sure as hell going to find out.

"What's that?"

"You tell me."

Hades shrugged and poured himself another shot of whiskey. "I've no fucking clue. I've never seen her before," he lied.

Poseidon's nostrils flared outward with anger. "We both know that's not true."

"How would you know?"

"Because I've seen the two of you together," Poseidon stated, his voice barely above a whisper.

Hades' blood ran cold. "Have you?"

His brother snatched the shot of whiskey out of his hand and downed it in one gulp. "Ever since news of her came to my attention, I've done my damnedest to discover everything I can about her."

"Which is?"

"Not much, unfortunately. But I did come across the

two of you in Central Park."

"And?"

Poseidon leaned close to him, his rancid breath blowing into Hades' face. "You're cheating on Persephone, aren't you?"

Hades stared back at him, looking appalled. "Fuck, no!"

"Come now, Hades. You don't have to keep it a secret. I won't tell."

He slammed down the newly filled shot, and turned to face Poseidon. His dark brown eyes grew darker until they were completely black in color.

"I'm not cheating on her, damn it!"

"Then why . . ."

He rubbed the bridge of his nose between a thumb and forefinger. "Artemis thinks the girl is the *Child of Calamity.*"

"Is she?"

"No."

"Are you sure?"

"Yes . . . No. I don't know. I sought the girl out to reassure myself that no harm came to her."

"You honestly don't think—"

"Yes, I do. Artemis is capable of just about anything when it comes to something she wants."

Poseidon frowned. "Our niece is the protector of young women. Surely, she wouldn't harm a hair on her head?"

"If it meant it would further her cause, I think she might."

"What would she want with the *Child of Calamity* anyway?"

"I don't know. Besides, you and I both know the child doesn't exist."

"What if the prophecy is no longer a lie?" Poseidon wondered. "What then?"

Hades drank his shot of whiskey, and opted to take another swig from the bottle. He didn't like the direction their conversation was going. The fact that another person now knew of Callidora's existence did not sit well with him.

How many more would come to know of her? he wondered. *What will happen once they put the pieces of the puzzle together?*

Unwilling to contemplate that very thought, Hades glared at Poseidon one last time before he teleported himself to the one place he knew he shouldn't go to– Medusa's private loft.

CHAPTER 14

Hades materialized in the middle of Medusa's kitchen, moments later. Her blue eyes narrowed as she assessed him from head to toe. He'd interrupted her cooking, and she was not too pleased with his doing so.

"Don't you ever knock?" Medusa barked as she tossed a stack of carrots down onto the counter.

"Not really."

She glared at him and pulled open a drawer to withdraw a sharp knife. "I'd prefer it. God knows Alexandros is mad at me because I flirt with you on occasion. I can't have him thinking you have free rein to come and go as you please."

Hades smirked and made his way to the breakfast nook. He pulled out one of its stools and promptly sat down, leaning his elbows across the counter's edge.

"But I do."

"That's beside the point."

"Having a bad day?"

"No," she breathed as she sliced through one of the carrots with more force than she'd intended.

"Are you sure?"

"Yes," she growled as several slices slid off the counter. She bent down to pick them up. "Bloody hell! Yes, damn you! Happy now?"

"No. Want to talk about it?"

Deep lines were etched around the corners of her mouth as she bit down on her lower lip. He watched as she rinsed the slices of carrots clean, and tossed them into a pot on the range nearby. She finished cutting up the rest of the carrots before reaching into the refrigerator to pull out several stalks of celery, four potatoes, a package of Beef Tripe, two radishes, an onion, and a handful of fresh parsley.

"You're making stew?" he prodded as she dropped everything on top of the counter.

"Yeah. Callidora has been craving beef stew for several days now. I thought I'd indulge her request."

The thought of his daughter warmed him from the inside-out. "How is she?"

She quickly peeled the potatoes, and chopped them up evenly. "Good. She's working at Kandie Kane's Emporium now."

"I know."

She paused her chopping to look up at him with surprise. "You do?"

"Yes."

"I see."

"Artemis knows, too, Edie," he admitted.

The knife clattered onto the kitchen counter. "Come again?"

"You heard me."

"How?"

"I'm not sure, though I suppose she's gone ahead and done a little digging of her own."

The blood drained from Medusa's cheeks. "D–Do you think she knows about me? About who I really am?" she asked, her voice barely a whisper.

"I doubt it, as she hasn't said a word about ever having seen someone like you before. She also strongly believes Callidora is the *Child of Calamity*."

"She's not, though."

Hades regarded her through veiled eyes. "What if she is?"

Medusa's reptilian eyes momentarily peeked through her glamour as anger flashed in their depths. "Hades . . ."

"Humor me. What if the prophecy is now true? What if your daughter is the one it speaks of?"

"She isn't."

"Edie . . ."

"No!" she hissed with vehemence.

Her glamour dropped completely, and she stood in front of him in all of her reptilian glory. Her body undulated back and forth, the snakes on her head snapping angrily in his direction. Hades admired the feral look on her face, immune to the curse Athena had bestowed upon her so long ago. In his eyes, she was as beautiful now as she was then. Granted, her body had changed in more ways than one, but it didn't change the way he saw and thought of her.

"You're angry, Love. I get it. But you must understand that there's more at stake here than we know. There are more who are coming to know of our daughter's existence. They, too, are convinced that she is the *Harbinger of Chaos and Destruction*. If we continue to ignore that fact, who knows what might happen then?" he reasoned.

Tears filled her eyes as she stared back at him. "But . . ."

He approached her and reached out to curl his hands around her face. The snakes lunged forward to sink their fangs into his flesh repeatedly. Ignoring the sting of their bites, he leaned forward to brush his lips across hers. Caught off guard, the snakes grew quiet, and lay limp across her head and face. He ended the kiss as quickly as it started and took a step back. The snakes eyed him warily, ready to strike at a moment's notice.

"I'm afraid the prophecy is now true. Whether or not Callidora is the one it speaks of remains to be seen. Greater forces now surround her, and we must do everything we can to protect her at all cost."

"You don't think—"

"I do. I honestly do. I'm not exactly sure as to who means well and who does not. Aside from Artemis, of course. But I do mean to discover that fact in due time. Though, I fear we don't have that much time on our side."

Several tears coursed down her cheeks. "Hades . . ."

He stepped forward once more to clasp her hands in

his. To his surprise, the snakes remained docile.

"I'll do everything I can to keep her safe."

Her lower lip trembled as she fought to keep her composure. "Promise?"

"Edie . . ."

"Say it!"

"I promise," he breathed, giving her hands a reassuring squeeze.

Come hell or high water, he'd do everything in his power to keep his daughter safe. He refused to allow Artemis to gain the upper hand in order to achieve an end to her own means. Whatever she was up to, he'd discover it soon enough. Then, and only then, would she come to know the full extent of his unholy wrath.

CHAPTER 15

Hades exited Medusa's apartment complex feeling a tad perplexed. His mind refused to make sense of the events that were now unfolding. Because of Artemis' snooping, a good many were now aware of the *Child of Calamity's* possible existence. Though he wasn't sure as to how many knew about the supposed prophecy, it would not be long until word got out.

Callidora's protection needed to be increased. He could not allow any harm to befall her. Alexandros would do everything he could to keep her safe, but he was the one who needed to ensure her safety. If need be, he could take her to the one place he knew of that would keep her existence hidden, once and for all. Though, he preferred to keep that option as a last resort.

Lost within his thoughts, he took no notice of a streak of black barreling in his direction until it was too late. The dark cloud lifted him into air, tossing his body along the invisible current. He howled with rage, summoning his powers so that he could set himself free, but the mass held tight onto him.

Higher and higher, they climbed until they loomed well above the city. The murky cloud hovered in the air as thin threads wrapped around Hades' wrists and ankles, spreading them apart. He writhed against his bindings as the dark mass swirled around him, tugging at his hair and flesh.

"Let go of me!" he demanded.

A bitter laugh erupted from the cloud's depths. "I don't think so."

"Alex?"

"I thought I made it clear that you were to stay away from Tasha?"

The hairs on the back of Hades' neck stood on end. The *God of Wrath* materialized in front of him in all of his resplendent glory. His blue eyes glowed with the fury boiling within him. The wind whipped his blond hair about his head, several strands falling into his eyes.

Like Zeus, Alexandros was able to manipulate thunder and lightning in any way, shape, or form. More often than not, he used both a means of signaling that he was near. Tonight, however, he meant to use both elements to inflict bodily harm.

Willing his powers to the surface, Hades broke free of his restraints moments before Alexandros threw a lightning bolt at him. He dodged the projectile and teleported himself behind the *God of Wrath*. In one smooth motion, he curled arm around his neck, yanking Alexandros' head back with more force than he'd intended. He cut off the god's airflow with the intent of subduing him.

Thwarting Hades' attempt, Alexandros' threw his head back, head-butting him across the nose. Bones crunched as he hit his mark. Hades howled with rage and released his hold on Alexandros. Blood spurted down his chin as he popped his nose back into place.

"Fucking hell!"

"That," Alexandros spat as he floated in the air nearby, "is for not doing as you're told."

"I had good reason!" he shot back in a nasal voice, spitting a wad of blood at his cousin's feet.

He deftly stepped aside and watched the congealed mass drift to the earth below. "Sure, you did."

"No, seriously, I did. This prophecy—the one concerning the *Child of Calamity* . . ." Hades replied as his voice returned to normal. "It doesn't bode well for any of us. Most especially Callidora."

Alexandros crossed his arms upon his chest, eyeing Hades with suspicion. "Go on."

"It's believed that Callidora belongs Zeus."

"I know that already."

"She's the supposed child spoken of in the prophecy."

"I know that, too."

"There are far too many of us who know about the *Child of Calamity*."

"So. What's it got to—?" Realization dawned in Alexandros' eyes. "*Oh*!?"

The weight sitting on Hades' shoulders lifted slightly.

"Yeah. She's not safe anymore."

"How long 'til people start putting things together?"

"It's hard to say."

"But . . . ?"

"We need to increase security around her."

"How?" Alexandros asked. "The more people we draw into this sordid circle, the more they're going to want a piece of the pie."

"Let me take care of them."

"Like you've taken care of things so far?"

Hades glared at him. "Shit's happened that's been out of my control. I've kept them safe for years, Alex. You can't fault me for trying to do what's right. Sooner or later, people are going to know Edie—*Medusa* is still alive. The least we can do is lessen the blow of the oncoming storm while protecting her and her daughter."

"Athena won't leave things as they are, you know."

"I know. She already suspects something."

Alexandros sighed and shook his head in dismay. "What now?"

"We go home."

"And?"

"Protect them, Alex. Shield them from what's coming as much as possible."

"What do you intend to do about all of this?"

Hades smiled, though it didn't quite reach his eyes. "I'm going to play clean up," he said, moments before he disappeared, leaving the *God of Wrath* to hover in the air while shaking his head at him.

CHAPTER 16

Landing lightly on his feet in front of his palace in Tartarus, Hades stared at the massive structure in contemplation. The lights were off in most of the rooms. The darkness lurking inside his home suited his mood. Everything was coming to a head for him, and he wasn't sure how much more of it he could take.

As *Lord of the Underworld*, he was in charge of making sure that the souls of the deceased were appropriately judged and sent to their rightful place. He was often considered to be a tyrant because he ruled the place with an iron thumb. Yet how could he not? He was a stickler for order, and everything was run to his liking.

His brow furrowed as he contemplated his current predicament. Persephone was gone, Medusa's whereabouts were soon to be known, much to his chagrin, and Artemis' machinations needed to be stopped. He wasn't sure as to what it was that his niece truly wanted, though he had an inkling of it.

It rankled him that she'd taken a shining to his daughter. The fact that she considered the girl to be the *Child of Calamity* further bothered him. Though, the more he thought about it, the more he started to believe that Callidora was the prophesized child. Granted, the prophecy itself had been a lie, forged at a moment when Zeus believed he'd lose control of the entire pantheon.

He understood Zeus' desperation, though he could not condone his actions. Because of one small lie, his life, Medusa's, his daughter's, and that of countless others, now lay in turmoil. He no longer doubted the fact that others would seek out the child the prophecy spoke of. How long that would take, he wasn't sure, but he would do everything he could to ensure that the backlash was minimal. His family's safety came first.

He'd promised Alexandros that he'd protect Medusa and his beloved child. That was a promise he intended on fulfilling in every way possible. He was grateful to his cousin in protecting Callidora. Yes, she wasn't his child by blood, but he'd taken her into his heart from the moment he'd laid eyes on her. That, in itself, spoke volumes. So much so, that he'd extended his protection to the lesser god, even though Alexandros hadn't wanted it in the first place.

The feel of an unexpected breeze sliding across his face broke through Hades' thoughts. Cerberus and his mate, Grahdea, towered overhead. Hades smiled and opened his arms wide as Cerberus bent his middle head to brush his tongue across his forehead. Grahdea joined in the venture, her tongues sliding across Hades' chin.

Soon, the hellhounds were rolling around, basking in Hades' attention.

"Hades?" Persephone replied as she spied her husband rolling around on the ground as he played with his monstrous pets.

Startled, Hades let go of Cerberus' right paw and sat up abruptly. "Persephone?"

"Yes?"

He stood up and brushed the dirt from his pants. "What are you doing here?"

She scowled at him and said, "This is my home, isn't it?"

"Yes."

"Then I can come and go as I please."

He nodded with understanding. "I thought you were staying at your mother's place."

"I was."

"But . . . ?"

She sighed softly, sliding her hands into the pockets of her faded jeans. "I missed being home. I've missed you," she admitted.

Hope flared within the depths of Hades' dark eyes. "You have?"

She smiled and took a step toward him. "Yes. This doesn't mean I accept what you've done, though. We still have to talk about that, you know."

"I know."

She wrapped her arms around his waist and pulled him to her. "I want to come home."

He reached up to curl his hands around her cheeks.

"You're always welcome here, Love," he whispered before claiming her lips with his.

She melted against him, responding to his kiss. The feel of her tongue sliding against his incited his passion. He wanted nothing more than to take her upstairs and make love to her, but he knew he needed to be patient. He'd dealt her a harsh blow with his admission about having an affair with Medusa. He needed to take his time and make it up to her. Whatever Persephone wanted, he'd give her. Her happiness meant more to him than his own.

She drew herself back to stare into his eyes. "Make love to me."

"Persephone . . ."

She reached down to cup his aching cock. "Please."

Without another word, he curled an arm beneath her legs and pulled her to him. He then teleported them to their bedroom. Gently placing her on her feet, he bent down to steal another kiss from her. She moaned, raking her fingers through the silky depths of his dark brown hair. He pulled her close, grinding himself against her, showing her just how much he wanted her.

Though, he wanted to ravish her, then and there, he needed to take his time. She'd gone through so much in so short a time. He needed her to trust him, to know that he did, indeed, love her. He would take his time with her, and show her just how much she meant to him. In time, she'd forgive him for what he'd done. He was sure of it.

For now, he was content to have her home again. She was the one woman he'd move heaven and earth for. The one woman who'd captured his heart from the moment he'd set eyes on her. Giving himself up to the emotions flowing within him, he swept his wife into his arms once more and lay her down across their bed, intent on loving her for as long as he was able.

CHAPTER 17

"*Daddy!*" *a voice whispered.*

The hairs on the back of Hades' neck rose with apprehension. Though he could not see her, he knew his daughter was somewhere nearby. A thick inky blackness surrounded him, preventing him from seeing where he was going. Snapping his fingers together, he produced a lantern and quickly lit it with another flick on his hand.

A sharp gasp slid past his lips as he eyed the carnage spreading out before him. Gods and goddesses were strewn across the path, their bodies torn into pieces. Blood and gore was spattered across the stone walls, slowly dripping to the ground below. The sight sickened him, but he knew there was nothing he could do for them.

"DADDY!" the child cried again. "Daddy, come save me!"

Callidora's voice grew frantic. He closed his eyes and threw out his power, trying to pinpoint her exact location. Yet he failed. A barrier prevented him from finding the one thing he loved the most.

Dear God, he thought. *Who's done this?*

He wanted to teleport himself home, to leave the gruesome sight behind. Unfortunately, he knew he couldn't. Something, or someone, had drawn him to the bowels of Tartarus, and he was intent on finding out what was going on.

A bright light erupted nearby, momentarily stealing his vision. Persephone materialized before him, her arms cradling her distended belly. Her eyes widened with horror as she stared at the bodies scattered across the tunnel's floor.

"What's going on?" she prodded, her voice barely a whisper.

"I'm not sure."

"Did you do this?"

He stared at her, appalled by the fact that she would think he was capable of doing such a thing. "No. I'd never—"

"DADDY! DADDY!"

She waddled over to him and laid a hand on his right shoulder. "Is that . . . ?"

"Callidora?"

"Yes."

"Yes, but I'm not exactly sure where she's at right now."

Persephone frowned. "You rule the Underworld, Hades. How can you not know where she is?"

"Something is preventing me from finding her."

"That's impossible!"

He shook his head and sighed once more. "Search for her, and you will see."

Taking a deep breath, she did as he asked. Her power rippled through the tunnel as she searched for the girl, but she found nothing that would lead her to Callidora. It was as if something kept her from doing so.

"I can't find her," she said, moaning aloud as the baby kicked within her.

Hades bent down to place the lantern on the floor before

straightening to wrap his arms around his pregnant wife. He placed a protective hand on her stomach as a wave of trepidation enveloped him. Deep inside, he knew what—or who—had caused this destruction. Yet he refused to believe it. There was no way such an innocent soul could take the lives of most of his brother's pantheon. Unless . . .

No! *he thought.* I can't think like that. I have to believe she's innocent. She wouldn't do this. I know she wouldn't!

"Hades?"

The sound of Persephone's soft voice broke through his thoughts.

"Hmmm."

She pointed toward the end of the tunnel. "There's something headed this way."

He gazed in the direction she pointed to, his blood roaring through his veins. A large cloud slowly crept along the corridor, shadowy threads spreading across the walls. It seemed to be searching for something, yet its intended prey was far out of its reach. Hades shoved Persephone behind him, intent on protecting her from what was coming. He refused to let any harm come to her and their child.

"We're going home."

She clutched his arms tight. "We can't."

"Yes, we can."

She shook her head back and forth with vehemence. "No. I've been trying to teleport myself out. Something's keeping me from doing so."

Hades pulled her to him and tried to orb them back to his palace. Nothing happened. They remained where they were standing as the oncoming shadow advanced upon them.

"Hades . . ."

He eyed the cloud, his mouth growing dry as it grew in size the more it crept toward them. He turned around and pulled his wife in the other direction, hoping to outrun whatever was coming at them. Persephone's moans grew stronger with every step.

Curling an arm beneath her legs, he hoisted her into his arms and hurried down the semi-darkened hallway, refusing to look behind him. Darkness soon enveloped them. Keeping a tight hold on Persephone, he pressed a hand against the cold stone wall and felt his way along. His wife's cries grew louder the farther along he walked.

"Damn it!"

"Hades, stop."

"I can't."

Another moan burst through Persephone's lips. "Please!"

He stopped within his tracks and gently placed Persephone on her feet. He produced another lantern, bathing the tunnel in a bright light. His eyes widened as he stared at a mound of bloodied body parts tucked into a corner of the tunnel. His wife cried out with fright as she, too, witnessed the carnage.

A loud roar thundered through the corridor behind them. They turned around to find the dark mass several inches away from them. Bright yellow eyes peered from its depths, flashing with anger. He pulled Persephone to him, prepared to defend her with every ounce of his being. The shadow advanced, thin tendrils creeping toward them. The sound of his wife's cries was the last thing he heard as the giant cloud enveloped them.

***

Hades awoke with an abrupt start. A cold sweat

erupted across his brow as he reached out to turn on the lamp on top of the bedside table. He groaned as the sudden glare stung his eyes. Glancing to his left, a sigh of relief escaped him as he gazed at a sleeping Persephone. She was safe and sound, oblivious of the world around her. He leaned forward to press a soft kiss to her right cheek before he slid out of bed.

Trudging across the room, he made his way to the bathroom. He turned the taps on the sink, and splashed the lukewarm water across his face. The dream had seemed so real, yet deep within his soul, he knew it wasn't. It was just a figment of his imagination. Callidora was no longer a child, and she didn't have the power to destroy the entire pantheon. Yes, she was a demigoddess, but her powers were nothing compared to what he'd seen in his dream.

What does it mean? he wondered. *Why am I seeing her in my dreams?*

His mind raced at about a mile-a-minute as he thought about what he'd seen. Everything felt so real. Persephone, the scattered body parts, the coldness of the tunnel—he'd even smelled the coppery scent of the blood itself. The sight of the shadowy creature heading for them was something he'd never seen before. Yes, he and his brethren created shadow beings on occasion to do their bidding, but never had anyone made one like the entity in his dream.

He leaned down to throw more water across his face, willing his mind to settle down. Yet nothing he thought about seemed to calm him down. The dream portended to something that had yet to come. The *Child of Calamity* existed. He knew that now, but he refused to believe that his daughter was the one the prophecy spoke of.

Artemis and the others are wrong. Callidora isn't the one. She's just a child for Pete's sake!

Growling with frustration, he turned off the taps with a quick flick of his hand. He grabbed the terry cloth towel hanging on the rack nearby and wiped his face dry. He dropped the towel in the sink and strode out of the bathroom, shutting off the lights behind him.

Zeus had mentioned that there were a good many that were now privy to the child's existence. Someone obviously knew the reason behind Artemis' fixation with the prophecy itself.

But who?

He made his way toward the bed. Hades gazed down at his sleeping wife, grateful of the fact that she had no inkling, whatsoever, of what was going through his mind. She looked so peaceful, so content, that he didn't have the heart to wake her. Instead, he bent down to brush a soft kiss across her cheek once more. She whimpered softly in her sleep, a smile darting across her lips.

God, she's beautiful! he thought as he straightened once more.

Taking one last look at Persephone's sleeping form, he walked out of his bedroom and headed for his study. Erratic thoughts tumbled through his head as he thought about the prophecy. It was then that he remembered the scroll Zeus had given him.

Marching over to his vault, he quickly unlocked it and pulled the scroll out. Unfurling the parchment, he smoothed it across his desk, and cast a quick spell to keep it flat on the desk's surface. He scowled as he leaned over the desk, taking a moment to fully examine the scroll's contents.

Zeus had written the prophecy in the center of the parchment with a graph detailing the pantheon's lineages painted below it. Along the margins, he'd noted each of the lesser gods and goddesses, along with loose mentions of the Titans. Upon closer examination, he also saw mention of several Egyptian and Atlantean gods, though there were several lines scratched through the names. Zeus, apparently, had cause in suspecting them of treachery against the pantheon.

Dear brother, these people don't know a thing about what goes on in our pantheon. I doubt they'd know about the prophecy itself. Why suspect these people of something they know not of? he wondered.

He dropped onto the chair behind the desk, running his hands through his already disheveled hair. A muscle twitched along his lower jaw as he tried to make sense of what transpired recently. His niece, Artemis, had unwittingly set many things into motion. She suspected that his daughter was the child the wretched prophecy spoke of, yet he refused to believe her claims. When the pantheon had first heard of the prophecy, it was believed that one of Zeus' numerous children would turn out to be the *Child of Calamity*. To think that another child could fit that role was ludicrous.

Hades manifested a box of magic markers, and pulled his chair closer to his desk. Grabbing a red marker, he highlighted Zeus and Hera's names in red. He capped the marker and grabbed a yellow one, drawing a yellow circle around Artemis' name. He jotted the words, *target #1*, in the center of it. He discarded the yellow marker, and grabbed a green one, circling Apollo's name. He then picked up the red marker, and drew a thin line between his name and his twin sister's. Beneath the line, he scrawled the word, *traitors*. Above Apollo's name, he wrote the word, *accomplice*, with a question mark at the end of it.

He grabbed the black marker and circled Deivos' name with it. He wrote the word, *traitor*, in the center of the circle. He bent over the parchment, carefully making notes across the vellum. By the time he was done, he'd noted everyone he suspected of being in cahoots with Artemis and her sordid plans. As he sat back in his chair, his gaze fell on the one name he hadn't given thought to in regards to his niece's shenanigans.

Leto . . .

Could it be? he thought as he scowled at the scroll lying on the desk in front of him. *Is it really that easy?*

He sat up and grabbed the black marker, etching three black lines under Leto's name. Beneath the lines, he wrote the words, *Mother of target #1, keep a close eye*, and highlighted the words in bright pink. Capping the marker, he tossed it across his desk and cracked his neck.

Hades was slowly coming to understand what drove Artemis to believe that Callidora was the *Child of Calamity*.

In her mind, she belonged to Zeus. She had no knowledge of Medusa's continued existence, so it was understandable that she thought such a thing. The girl was an unknown and could have been one of his brother's numerous illegitimate children.

He knew, then, that he needed to sway Artemis from such thoughts. His daughter's safety was in question, and he refused to allow his niece to harm the one thing he loved the most. Granted, Persephone was his first, and true, love, but it was his daughter who held a special place in his heart.

He needed to make everyone believe that Callidora was not the child the prophecy spoke of. Such a feat was going to take some doing, but he knew it had to be done. Somewhere out there, the child did, indeed, exist. He was determined to find him or her, and bring the child to everyone's attention. The sooner, the better. Taking his niece's attention off of his daughter was a necessity, as was keeping Medusa's existence a secret.

Standing up, he re-rolled and sealed the scroll. He penned Persephone a quick note, sighing with dismay. The thought of leaving her to take care of the matter at hand during such a crucial moment in their relationship sat ill with him, but he knew it needed taking care of. In time, she'd forgive him.

He produced a red rose and set it down beside the letter he'd written, knowing that his wife would find it soon enough. With one last look around the room, he teleported himself to Mount Olympus, determined in seeking out the one woman who could lay these protected secrets to rest–*Leto.*

THE CHILD OF CALAMITY SERIES
BOOK 3

Hidden
Secrets

LISSETTE E. MANNING

Sometimes, some secrets are better left unknown.

From the moment Artemis brought news of the *Child of Calamity* to his attention, Apollo's life has never been the same. Though he's not exactly sure if Callidora Spiros is truly what his sister says she is, he's willing to give the girl the benefit of a doubt. After all, the young woman is beautiful, and draws him in like a moth to a flame.

Though Zeus rules Mount Olympus with an iron thumb, Apollo knows that his father's reign may some day come to a close. The events his sister set into motion threaten the very fabric of the world they live in. His sister has decreed that her every wish be fulfilled, and she'll do everything possible to make sure things go her way.

Life soon takes a different turn as further secrets come to light. His sister will not be deterred from the task at hand. Apollo soon realizes that the prophecy may come to pass no matter what he or anyone else does to stop it. Nevertheless, he'll do everything possible to thwart his sister's every goal.

CHAPTER 1

Apollo growled with frustration as he walked along, his blue eyes blazing with suppressed fury. He couldn't believe Artemis had easily dismissed his willingness to help her. Granted, he wasn't that familiar with the prophecy she'd spoken of, but that didn't mean he was that clueless about the world around him. He'd decided to give her a day or two to come around, but the days had come and gone with no word from her.

She'd piqued his curiosity in regards to the girl in the photograph she'd shown him. At nineteen years of age, the young woman was a sight to behold with her lustrous blue-black hair and vivid cornflower blue eyes. She was a woman that drew a man's interest in more ways than one. To his astonishment, he now wanted to know more about her.

He slid his hands into the pockets of his jeans, his brow dipping low as he thought about the girl and the prophecy. *How had Artemis come across it in the first place?* he wondered. *Why is it so important that she have this girl under her wing?*

Those questions and more tumbled through his mind as he walked along. He couldn't help but to wonder what his sister was getting him into. Whatever it was, he knew he couldn't walk away from it.

Artemis' memory was embedded deep within his soul. She was his twin, his confidant, and so much more. Their sordid relationship had begun as a result of having to band together in order to save their mother time and time again. Back then, they'd had no one to see them through the hectic ordeals they'd faced. The twins had done the only thing they could have done in such times of hardship. They'd turned to each other, and now the rest was history.

And now, here I am doing yet another favor for the bitch, he thought ruefully.

He loved Artemis. There was no question about that, but sometimes, she got on his nerves. Most especially when she exerted her holier-than-thou attitude over him. He understood the fact that she was older than him. She'd gone through so much more than he had before he'd been born. In a sense, she was like a surrogate mother to him, since she'd helped their mother birth him. Yet he preferred not to think about that fact too much. Doing so allowed him to see Artemis in a much different light.

Apollo slid his hands into the pockets of his jeans, taking in the bright flashing lights of the big city. New York was one of his favorite places to be, most especially at night. He was able to blend into the crowd, and give in to his baser desires often. Man or woman, he didn't care as long as his passions were satisfied time and again. Granted, none held a candle to Artemis, but that was something that couldn't be helped.

He shook his head to clear it, wishing that thoughts of his sister didn't follow him everywhere he went. She was like a thorn in his side. No matter how much he tried to forget about her, she was always there.

Focusing his thoughts on the picture his sister had shown him, he manifested an exact copy of the photograph. He snatched the glossy paper out of the thin air as it hovered nearby. The sight of the girl's face taunted him. His sister's latching on to the girl might have been an accident, but there was no denying that young woman was extraordinary.

The look of determination on her face had been captured perfectly on film. Though she smiled, her eyes spoke a different story. They seemed sad, a little too sad. He couldn't help but to wonder as to what had marred her happiness at that given moment. Apollo would have given anything to brighten up her day, then and there.

He took a deep breath and shoved the picture into the right pocket of his jeans. Now was not the time to worry about such things. Apollo needed something to quell the rampant thoughts tumbling through his mind. Sex, drugs, booze–he didn't care as long as it took his mind off of Artemis and the matter at hand. Striding into the nearest establishment, he grinned as the loud music and strobing lights drew his attention.

This will do perfectly, he thought as he pushed through the crowd and made his way toward the nearest bar.

CHAPTER 2

The scent of alcohol assailed Apollo's nostrils the closer he got to the bar. A bartender caught his eye, smiling with appreciation as his gray eyes roved up and down the god's immaculately dressed form. He smirked with delight and winked at the man. Sliding onto the nearest bar stool, he watched the guy make his way over.

"What can I get ya?" he asked.

Apollo grinned and leaned his elbows across the counter's edge. "What do you have?"

The bartender smiled. "Depends on what yer looking for."

He licked his lips and tilted his head to the side. "I'll have a Jägermeister, if you carry the stuff."

"Why wouldn't we?"

"Not all places do."

His companion laughed and set a full glass down in front of him. "Ya, well, we do. Anything else I can get ya?"

Apollo shook his head. "Nope," he said, and knocked back his drink in one gulp.

The bartender shook his head, displeased with Apollo's sudden disinterest, and turned to another of his customers. The god grinned as he placed the glass down on the counter. He loved messing with mortal's minds, and this was one such0 occasion. There was no doubt in his mind that the man would have given him exactly what he wanted. Yet that wasn't what he was looking for. At least, not yet.

"You're not lookin' to drink yourself into oblivion, are you?" a condescending voice inquired.

He turned toward the newcomer and shook his head. "Maybe. What the fuck are you doing here?"

His half-brother, Dionysus, stood in front of him dressed in a pair of torn jeans, a paint spattered white t-shirt, black fingerless gloves, and black combat boots. His black hair was streaked with purple. If he hadn't known any better, he'd have assumed the *God of the Grape Harvest and Wine-Making* was just some ordinary kid trying to be both artistic and Goth at the same time. Dionysus was known for his random ways and loved to keep people guessing as to who and what he was really like.

Taking a seat, Dionysus ordered himself a Mojito, before addressing Apollo. "Looking for some excitement."

Apollo summoned the bartender once more. The bartender quickly refilled his glass, leaving the bottle of Jägermeister behind before he moved away once more. He grabbed the glass and brought it to his lips, taking a hefty gulp of his drink.

"Funny, so am I."

"Ain't that a coincidence!"

He lowered the glass and stared at his half-brother in contemplation. "What do you want, Dio?"

"Nothing."

"Yeah, and pigs can fly."

"They can," Dionysus said. "Strap on a pair of Hermes' winged boots to one, and they'll go anywhere."

"You rang?" Hermes inquired as he materialized beside the pair.

Apollo groaned and downed the rest of his drink. Tonight wasn't going the way he'd expected it to. He grabbed the bottle and poured himself another drink, reaching into his pocket for some of the money he'd stashed there earlier. The photograph drifted to the floor as he pulled out several bills. He slapped several down on the counter's surface, and swore vehemently as he bent to pick it up.

Dionysus picked it up instead and glanced at the image. "Who's she?"

"Don't know."

Hermes leaned over his half-brother's shoulder and whistled softly. "She's mighty fine. I'd tap that!"

Apollo's left arm swung out and belted Hermes across his chest. "Have you no decency?"

"Hell no. I'm the *God of Transitions and Boundaries*, brother. Some also say I'm a thief. Can't forget I'm *God of the Herds*, too. And . . ."

Dionysus glared at Hermes with derision. "You're

the bloody messenger of the gods, you wanker! Friggin'
ass-kisser, too, if I may say so."

"Yeah, well—"

"Dude!" Apollo said. "Chill. What are you guys
doing here anyway? Don't you have shit to do?"

"Besides follow you?" Hermes asked as he sat down
to the left of Apollo.

"Follow me?"

The bartender set a large glass of beer down in front
of Hermes, glancing at the trio with curiosity. Apollo gave
him a scathing look, and he moved away without another
glance in their direction.

Hermes drew the glass to him. "Your sister's up to
no good."

Apollo's mouth grew dry. "My sister?"

"Come now, brother. Surely, you've heard?"

Fuck me! Damn you, Artemis!

"About?"

Dionysus cleared his throat and leaned toward him.
"She's consortin' with Deivos, man."

Apollo froze as he lifted his newly refilled glass to his
lips. His mind went blank. He hadn't heard his half-
brother's words right, had he?

"Say what?"

"I said—"

"I heard you."

"Then why—"

"'Cause I thought I heard you wrong. And you're
mistaken. She wouldn't. Not with him."

Hermes laughed and slapped his hand across the

counter's surface. "Wait! You thought it was something else?"

He felt his cheeks grow warm as Hermes' laughter intensified. *Yep, tonight definitely went to shit!* he thought with irritation.

When it came to Artemis, it was hard to know exactly what she was up to. This time, however, he was privy to something they didn't know a thing about. Which made Dionysys' declaration all the more startling.

There's no fucking way she'd . . . No! Just . . . NO!

Without uttering another word, he flashed himself out of the club, leaving his half-brothers to their own devices. There was no way in hell he was going to listen to anything else they said. The thought of Artemis consorting with his cousin made him feel sick to his stomach. It wiped all thought of her and the *Child of Calamity* from his mind.

Surely, my sister hasn't sunk so low? he wondered, and set off in the direction of Deivos' penthouse.

CHAPTER 3

The door to his cousin's penthouse blew open. Apollo stepped through the mangled doorway, taking pleasure in the fact that he'd destroyed it. He fumbled in the darkness for a light switch, cursing loudly as he stumbled across several planks of wood. He finally found it and stared at the mess he'd made. Broken pieces of wood and furniture were scattered in every direction.

He made his way further into the room, waiting for his cousin to appear. There was no way Deivos could not have heard the explosion. Yet no one came as he waited. He heard nothing aside from his own breathing.

Growling with frustration, he raised a hand with the sole intent of clearing the mess. Dionysus' words rose to the surface, however, and he left things as they were. Deivos would not be happy once he got home.

The glimmer of something in the distance caught his eye as he turned to leave. Moving toward the object, a sharp gasp slid past his lips as he stared down at a table laden with photographs, jewelry, dirty clothes, books, and an assortment of video games. By the looks of it, Deivos was hoarding someone else's valuables.

But why? he wondered.

He soon found the answer to his question as he picked up a copy of a photograph he'd come to know so well. The picture fluttered to the table as he picked up another. Apollo's hackles rose with apprehension as he riffled through the stack of photographs. His cousin was tracking the girl and keeping a very good eye on her from the looks of it. That much was evident as he sifted through the images.

Dropping the stack onto the table, he picked up several of the video game cartridges. *The Last of Us, Assassin's Creed: Brotherhood, Star Ocean: The Last Hope, The Fast and the Furious, Need for Speed*—the titles were endless. Did they belong to Deivos? Or the girl, perhaps?

He moved on to a small pile of jewelry, and carefully examined each piece. A golden heart with a ruby embedded in its middle caught his attention. Rubbing the pad of his thumb across its surface, he pocketed the necklace, and reached for a dingy gray-colored sweater. Before he could pick it up, the sound of the elevator doors opening and closing alerted him to Deivos' arrival.

Apollo masked his presence and watched as his cousin came to a stop in front of the broken doorway. Several angry epitaphs slid past Deivos' lips as he surveyed the damage. He grinned as he watched the demigod sift through the door's remnants.

Deivos' right hand hovered above the broken wood

for a minute or so. He turned toward the doorway and flicked his hand at it. Apollo watched as the pieces flew into the door's frame and sealed themselves together. The door soon stood before them in one piece. Not a single crack was visible.

"'Ad fun, did ya?" Deivos asked as he turned in Apollo's direction.

The *God of Light* pursed his lips, intent on keeping his presence hidden, but his cousin surprised him. The shield surrounding him shimmered before it disappeared completely. A crooked smile tilted the corner of Deivos' mouth as Apollo appeared in front of him, moments later.

"What the–?"

"A gift from my father, mate. I can detect a god or goddess if they're nearby."

"Poseidon gave you that ability?"

"Yep."

"But . . . Why?"

"Why not?" Deivos brushed past him and made his way over to the mini bar. "It's come in 'andy, so far."

"I can see that," Apollo said with annoyance.

"Found what yer lookin' fer?"

"Not exactly."

Deivos lifted the glass he'd filled with a shot of Bourbon to his lips, gulping half of its contents down. "Coulda fooled me. 'At table ain't exactly 'ow I'd left it."

Embarrassment clouded Apollo's features. *Damn him!* he thought. *He's more astute than I've given him credit for.*

"I was curious, that's all."

His cousin's eyes narrowed as he set the glass down on the bar's counter. He strode over to the table and rummaged through it in search of something. Apollo bit down on the left corner of his mouth, hoping Deivos wouldn't notice that anything was missing.

"Where is it?"

"Where's what?"

Deivos turned to face him, his hazel eyes dark with anger. "The necklace."

Apollo shrugged. "I've no idea what you're talking about."

"Yeah, ya do. The golden 'eart with a ruby in its middle. It was 'ere 'fore I left. No one's been in 'ere 'til now."

"You don't know that. Anyone could have—"

"'Course, I do. The wards I cast on it, they're gone."

Apollo frowned. "Wards?"

"Yep. Pops showed me 'ow to make 'em. Thin' is, I can't pick up on 'em. Somethin's messin' with my mojo."

"Your mojo?" Apollo laughed. "Dude, you sound like that guy from that movie. What's the name of it? Damn it!"

"Ya so much as—"

"Austin Powers! The bloke was always going on about his mojo. That shit doesn't exist. You know that, right?"

"Nay, mate. Yer wrong there. We're not talkin' about 'at, though. Where's the necklace?" Deivos asked once more as he summoned a burst of power.

The gold heart stashed in Apollo's pocket started to

warm up. A muscle twitched along his jaw as he realized that Deivos was trying to get a reading on the necklace's location. Though he was tempted to shove his hands into his pockets and draw the necklace out, he ignored the notion. He used a subtle burst of power instead, and sent the necklace home, conveniently dropping it into a coffer sitting on his desk. His cousin growled, a look of contempt spreading across his face.

"Ya took it, didn't ya?"

"Now, Deivos . . ."

"Screw ya! Yoo've no right to take what ain't yers, Apollo."

"I've done no—"

Deivos barreled into him, pinning him to the wall behind him. "Fuck ya! What'd ya do wit' it?"

"I told you—"

A sharp jab to his ribs cut off his reply. Deivos prepared himself to deliver another blow. Apollo saw it coming and sidestepped his advance. His cousin plowed into the wall, causing the plaster to crack in several places.

"Why is it important?"

"It's none of ya business. It's mine, plain an' simple."

Gathering a hold of himself, Deivos turned and launched himself at Apollo once more. He zapped himself across the room, grinning with amusement as his cousin tripped and fell across the wooden coffee table.

"Now, now," Apollo said. "We both know it's not yours."

Deivos pushed himself into a sitting position, mumbling angrily. "So?"

"So, how about you give me some answers, and I'll see about giving it back to you."

CHAPTER 4

Deivos' eyes narrowed as he stared at Apollo, trying to deduce his intentions. "What do ya wanna know?"

Apollo held out his hand and summoned the necklace. He dangled the pendant in front of him, watching it swirl back and forth in the air.

"Who does this belong to?"

A muscle twitched along Deivos' jaw as he glanced at the necklace. "A woman."

"I gathered that much. The question is, who?"

"Ya don't know 'er."

"I don't?"

"No, but . . ."

"Yes?"

"Yer sister 'as an inklin'."

A light bulb went off inside Apollo's head. "The *Child of Calamity*?"

His cousin's eyes widened. "Artemis told ya about 'er?"

"Sort of."

Deivos pushed himself to his feet and ran an unsteady hand through his brown hair. "What do ya mean sort of?"

Apollo sent the necklace back to its previous location, and drew the photograph out of his pocket. He sent it spinning through the air in Deivos' direction. His cousin caught it in midair and frowned. A muscle twitched along his lower jaw as he stared at it.

"Artemis gave this to ya?" he asked as he held the picture aloft.

"Not quite," Apollo said as he grabbed the glossy paper and stowed it in his pocket once more.

Deivos' eyes narrowed. "Ya stole it?"

"No. It's a copy, you moron. Now, tell me what I want to know."

"Ya 'aven't asked anythin'."

Apollo crossed his arms around his chest and waited. Deivos sighed with frustration and pointed to the leather sofa.

"'Ave a seat."

"What for?"

"Ya want to know, don't cha?"

Apollo's face grew warm. "Oh. Yes."

"Want anythin' to drink?"

"Nope. I'm good."

Deivos strode over to the mini bar once more. "I need a drink."

"Summon one."

"Damned wankers," Deivos said with irritation.

"Always takin' the easy road. Ain't nothin' like the real thin', ya know."

"Everything we conjure up is real. You know that as well I do."

Deivos tossed back his drink. "Yeah, but . . . Fuck, nev'r mind. Ask yer damned questions, an' get the 'ell outta 'ere."

The left corner of Apollo's mouth twitched slightly. "Who is she?"

"I don't know."

"You don't know?"

"No," Deivos said, his voice a tad lower than normal.

"You're lying."

His cousin looked up, his eyes boring into his. "Even if I did know, I wouldn't tell ya. Ya didn't 'ire me."

Realization dawned on Apollo. "But Artemis did."

Deivos shrugged. "Maybe. Maybe not."

"The two of you suspect she's the *Child of Calamity*, though. That's why you're always so evasive. You're protecting Artemis' interests."

"There's no way to be sure of 'at. Not yet."

"But you aim to find out."

"Tryin' to. She—"

"Yes?"

Deivos shook his head to clear it. "Nothin'. I've said enough."

"You haven't said anything!"

"I've said more than I should. Yoo've no idea—"

Apollo stood up. "I've an idea about a good many

things, cousin. You, included. So until you're ready to talk, I think I'll hold on to that necklace," he said, and orbed himself back to Mount Olympus.

CHAPTER 5

Apollo dropped onto his bed, summoning the necklace he'd taken from Deivos to him. He stared at the gold heart with the embedded ruby for several minutes, trying to make sense of it.

Who does it belong to, and what does my cousin want with it? Could this be linked to the child? he wondered.

He turned the delicate pendant around, and caught sight of an inscription embedded into the precious metal. Apollo leaned forward and squinted his eyes. The small letters were a tad hard to see. A quick burst of power remedied that, however. Rolling onto his back, he watched the hologram he'd created expand before him.

Harbinger of Chaos and the Destroyer of Worlds

His heart raced as the familiar words sank in. He no longer doubted that the jewelry was linked to the child itself. Deivos knew more than he let on. Yet Deivos' hoarding articles that belonged to a woman who might not even be the prophesized child didn't make sense. Did he plan to use them against the gods? Was he also planning to take Zeus' golden throne and make it his own?

Apollo sat up and glared at the necklace. He sent it to his vault, rubbing his hands against his jean-covered thighs. His mind roiled with the implications of what he'd seen at Deivos' apartment. There was no telling what his cousin meant to do with the articles he'd gathered. The demigod was up to something, though he wasn't sure as to what his plans truly were.

Artemis soon appeared at the foot of his bed before he had a chance of pondering the notion. She wore a white silk dress that hugged her curves to perfection. Her fiery mane was pulled into a tight chignon, several errant curls framing her face. A sardonic smile danced across her lips.

"Something wrong?" she asked as she sat down on the edge of his bed.

He drew himself up against the wooden headboard, staring at her through heavy-lidded eyes. "Perhaps."

"Want to talk about it?"

"Not really."

She chuckled and shook her head. "But . . . ?"

"There is no but."

Artemis picked at the gathered folds of the quilt she sat on, a slight frown marring her forehead. "I beg to differ."

"What do you want, Artemis?"

"I came to check on you," she said, bestowing him with a covert look as she looked at him from the corner of her eye.

"Why?"

"Why not?"

He crossed his arms about his chest and rolled his eyes at her. "You never do anything without a purpose."

She feigned a pout. "Can't I come see you once in awhile?"

All thoughts fled as he stared into her silvery-yellow orbs. The desire lurking in their depths told him exactly what she wanted. Artemis crawled across the bed and slid onto his lap. She leaned forward to brush her lips across his, nipping gently at his lower lip. Apollo reacted and wrapped his hands around her waist. His cock throbbed with anticipation. She jerked her hips and rubbed herself against him. A strangled moan escaped him.

"Stop!"

Artemis stopped moving and pulled herself back to gaze down at him. "You don't want this?"

"No. Yes. Fuck, I don't know!"

Apollo pushed her off his lap and slid off the bed. He ran an unsteady hand through his blond hair as he made his way toward the panoramic window on the leftmost wall. Her warm touch was wreaking havoc on his libido.

They'd engaged in sexual pursuits often in the past, giving each other what they needed in more ways than one. If Zeus hadn't exiled their mother so long ago, none of what they'd done would have happened. They probably would have lived different lives. Perhaps they'd have gotten along better than they did now.

We certainly wouldn't have become lovers, he mused.

No? Artemis asked as she walked up to him.

He stiffened as she wrapped her arms around his waist, tucking her chin against the hollow of his left shoulder. *Get out of my head.*

You know I can't do that.

Yes, you can.

She snorted and nipped at the soft flesh. *I don't want to.*

You have to.

Artemis slid her hands downward, cupping his aching manhood. *Where's the fun in that?*

Why are you here?

I've told you—

You've said nothing, Sister.

I've come to see you.

Bullshit!

She squeezed his jean-covered cock and grinned as he inhaled sharply. *I'm hungry, brother.*

Are you?

Uh-huh.

Apollo disengaged himself from her embrace and strode back toward the bed. He dropped onto it and glared at her.

"Why are you really here?"

She sighed and turned to face him. "You miss nothing, do you?"

"You're my twin. I notice everything."

"I'd rather you didn't."

"Yeah, well, I do. Now, what is it you want?"

"You've something of mine."

"I do?"

"Yes, and I want it back."

His eyes narrowed. "And what would that be?"

"The necklace, brother. Give it to me."

"Necklace?"

"Don't play coy with me. I know you have it. Deivos—"

A muscle twitched along his jaw. "Deivos, what?"

She pulled herself up to her full height of five-feet-eight inches tall. "Never you mind. I want the necklace, so hand it over."

"It doesn't belong to you."

"Yes, it does."

"No, it doesn't. But you know whose it is, don't you?"

Her face paled as she stared back at him. "I—No."

"You're lying, Artemis."

"Apollo . . ."

"Is it hers?"

"Who's?"

"Callidora's."

She shrugged nonchalantly. "I don't know."

"You do. So does Deivos. You really are convinced she's the *Child of Calamity*, aren't you?"

Artemis licked her lips and avoided his intense scrutiny. "I—Maybe."

Apollo pushed himself off the bed, and made his way

toward her. "What if she's not what you think she is?"

"She is!" she whispered.

He grasped her shoulders and shook her slightly. "She's not."

She blinked away the sudden rise of her tears. "She is, Apollo. That's why I've come for that necklace, so hand it over."

"I can't," he said, and let go of her. "Until I get the right answers to the questions running through my head, I'm holding on to it. I'm tired of these fucking secrets. Someone knows something, and I intend on uncovering what I need to know. With or without your help!"

He left her behind as he transported himself to his mother's favorite hideaway.

CHAPTER 6

"Apollo?" Leto asked as he appeared in the middle of the courtyard. "What are you doing here?"

Apollo tugged at the collar of his tunic and turned around to face his mother. "I need a bit of counsel."

Leto frowned. "In regards to?"

"I think you know why I'm here, Mother."

Her mouth thinned to a tight line. "I thought we'd gone over this."

"Have we?"

"I don't understand."

"You know more about the *Child of Calamity* than you let on, don't you?"

She sighed with discontent. "Darling, I–"

The look he gave his mother silenced her. "Help me to understand why my sister seems to be fixated on a mere prophecy, Mom. Artemis keeps giving me the run around whenever I try to delve further into things. She's in cahoots with Deivos, too. Did you know about that?"

Leto tilted her head at him in contemplation. Her dark eyes were full of sadness as she gazed at him. A soft sigh escaped her.

"Let's go inside."

"Why?"

"Privacy, dearest."

"Surely, we have that here?"

"I think not. There are prying eyes and avid ears everywhere, all eager to do harm. Come. Let's convene within my personal chamber."

Apollo followed her inside, his brow furrowing with every step he took. He no longer doubted that his mother knew more about the situation than he did. The look in her eyes had told him so. His pulse raced as he thought about what she would soon tell him.

Will she be able to shed more light on the child itself? What secrets will she divulge to me?

His wayward thoughts were interrupted as Leto closed to the door of her room once he'd walked inside. She pointed to a circle of chairs she'd erected in front of the marble fireplace and nodded. He understood her silent request and moved to take a seat.

His mother approached the mahogany table she kept stocked with assorted fruits, cheeses, meats, and wine. Her hands moved about as she prepared a plate for them, pouring healthy portions of the wine into two goblets. Once satisfied, she placed everything on the coffee table in front of Apollo. She sat down and gave him a tentative smile.

"What would you like to know?"

Apollo leaned back against the cushioned seat, his blue eyes troubled. "How much more do you know about the child?"

"Quite a bit."

"Artemis told you?"

"No."

"Then, how?"

She sighed once more and closed her eyes. Leto summoned forth the ancient scroll she'd viewed not too long ago. Her heart raced as she realized she was committing a grievous sin in removing it from the grand library, and prayed that Zeus would forgive her for doing so.

Apollo watched as she pushed aside the plate of food and spread the scroll open across the table. Her hand hovered above it for a minute or so. It laid flat, its content ready for his prying eyes.

"Read it," she said, and settled back into her chair.

He frowned and leaned forward to peruse the document. At first, the words he read made no sense to him. His mind refused to understand their meaning until the moment of clarity came to him. Apollo looked up, his eyes wide with fear.

"W–What is this?" he whispered.

"The prophecy."

"The one Artemis . . ."

"The one she told you about, yes."

"S–So the child . . ."

"It exists."

"The girl . . . Is she . . . ?"

"We–I don't know."

"Artemis thinks so."

"She could be mistaken," his mother said. "For all we know, the child could be male."

"Do you think it is?"

Leto shrugged. "It's hard to say."

"Mom . . ."

She raised a hand to silence him. "What did Artemis promise you in exchange for helping her with this sordid quest?"

Apollo's face paled. "I don't see what this has to do with–"

"It has everything to do with this. Don't you see? She's using you."

"Am I?" Artemis asked as she materialized before them, her silvery-yellow eyes full of hatred as she stared at her mother.

"Artemis!" Leto gasped.

Her daughter crossed her arms about chest, tapping her foot with impatience. "What have you told him?"

"Nothing. Yet."

"I forbid you from doing so."

Leto rushed to her feet, her right knee banging against the side of the table. The goblets toppled over, causing the wine to drip to the floor. Apollo hurried to wipe away the mess, keeping his attention on his mother and sister as he did so.

"You have no say in what I can or can't do."

Artemis' chin rose with determination. "I do when it concerns me."

"He has a right to know!"

"Yes, he does, but not until I deem him ready."

"Why not?"

"Because I say so!" She glanced at Apollo. "Our deal is off!"

She disappeared, leaving him feeling a tad confused.

"Well, that went well," he said.

Leto turned to face him. "I'm sorry. I—"

He shrugged. "I wouldn't worry, Mother. She'll reinstate our agreement once she's calmed down."

She took a step toward him and placed a hand on his forearm. "Whatever it is she wants, let it go."

"I can't, Mother."

"You can. For our sake, and that of the pantheon, you must!"

"How? Perhaps what she plans to do may better the state of our own affairs."

She frowned. "What does she plan to do?"

"I can't tell you."

"Apollo . . ."

"I'm sorry, Mother," he said, and zapped himself home.

CHAPTER 7

"It took you long enough," Artemis replied as he appeared in the middle of his bathroom.

Apollo turned around. "What are you doing here?"

She strode inside, the door swinging closed behind her. "You're so predictable."

His mouth dropped open with surprise. "You're not mad?"

"No."

"But . . ."

Artemis grinned and reached out to place her hands upon his chest. "Oh, please. That was all for show."

"Mother thinks–"

She placed a finger across his lips. "Let her think what she wants. No one needs to know what we're up to."

He nipped at the tip of her finger and took a step back. "What are we up to?"

"Revolution."

"How? We haven't done anything to move things forward."

"You haven't, but I have."

"Such as?"

She smiled. "I can't divulge my secrets, brother. God knows who you'd tell!"

"I haven't—"

Her smile vanished. "You almost told Mom what I'm up to."

"I did not!"

"Why were you with her, then?"

"I seek understanding, Artemis. I'm tired of these games. You've set things into motion that are far beyond our means. This child . . . The prophecy is not something to be trifled with."

"The prophecy doesn't lie, Apollo."

"Yes, but—"

"Father must be impeached. His callous ruling of Olympus must be stopped. Our people should be given a chance to—"

A bolt of lightning shattered the roof above them, sinking deep into the marble floor as bits of stone tumbled all around them. Artemis' face paled as she realized Zeus was near. He appeared before them, his blue eyes burning with anger. She stepped away from him, afraid of what her father would do to her.

"What lies are you tellin' about me?" he asked, his mouth curled into a sneer.

"Lies?"

"I heard what you said."

She gathered her composure and stood up straight. "It's true!"

"I rule as I see fit."

"You impart injustice whenever possible, Father, but we shouldn't have to bend to your demands."

"You and the rest of our pantheon will do as I say."

"We will not. The time will come when—"

His eyes narrowed with suspicion. "When what?"

A knowing smile danced across Artemis' lips. "You'll see," she said, and dematerialized.

Zeus turned around to face his son. "What have you been doin'?"

Apollo feigned ignorance. "Nothing."

"I beg to differ."

He held up his hands in supplication. "I swear it, Father. You know how Artemis is when something takes her fancy."

"And I'm in her line of fire. Is that it?"

"Apparently."

A muscle twitched along Zeus' lower jaw. "Your mother put her up to this, didn't she?"

"No. How could she? I don't even know what my sister is up to, much less Mother."

Disapproval clouded Zeus' face. "So help me, Apollo, if I find out you're consortin' with your sister, I'll—"

"You'll what?"

"There will be hell to pay!"

His father popped out of existence, leaving him alone to ponder his words. Confusion reigned within him as he tried to make sense of what had transpired. He'd gone to his mother for further understanding in regards to the *Child of Calamity*. Instead, he was left with more questions than before.

Artemis' machinations were growing by the second. She was determined to leave him out of the loop. That much was apparent. He needed to unlock the secrets surrounding the child and the prophecy itself, but he wasn't sure as to whom he could trust in order to do so. His mother knew, but she wasn't that forthcoming. She was more interested in learning of his sister's plans. Zeus . . . well, he wasn't too happy about his ties to Artemis. Artemis wasn't talking, and his cousin's help was also out of the question.

What can I do? he wondered. *Who can I trust with the little I know?*

Apollo reached out to curl his hands around the edge of the sink. His knuckles whitened as the fury he'd suppressed within him rose to the surface. There were so many secrets to unlock that he wasn't sure where to begin. Granted, the necklace he now had in his possession gave him a slight leverage, but it did nothing to lessen his frustrations.

Part of him knew that he'd find the answers to his questions soon enough. He needed to wait until that moment came. Patience, however, was never one of his virtues.

Straightening to his full height of five-feet-eight inches tall, Apollo stared at his reflection in the mirror. A slight sneer curled the right corner of his mouth. If he had to wait until then, he was going to enjoy himself in doing so. With or without his sister's presence by his side.

CHAPTER 8

Several hours later, Apollo found himself strolling through the gardens of his estate. Though he wasn't prone to doing such a thing, he needed a suitable means to clear his mind. His head ached as he thought about Artemis and everything she'd set into motion. He was beginning to understand how such a prophecy could wreak havoc on people's lives.

Artemis planned on taking their father's throne as her own. The wretched prophecy was her ticket in getting there. Granted, he wasn't quite sure as to how she'd achieve such a feat. Sure, the events she'd set into motion were slowly turning the tides in her favor, but she wasn't quite that forthcoming with what she was doing. The bits and pieces she divulged to him weren't adding up. If he was going to beat her at her own game, he needed to understand what was driving her to do what she was doing.

But how?

Deivos hadn't told him much either, though he'd subtly hinted at certain things. He was now convinced that the necklace belonged to Callidora. Apollo also surmised that the other items he'd come across at Deivos' apartment also belonged to the girl. None of what he'd seen explained as to what his cousin planned to do with everything, however.

Could it be . . . ? he wondered as a light bulb went off in his head once more. *Nah. It can't be that easy. Can it?*

Apollo sat down on one of the marble benches scattered throughout the garden. He summoned the necklace to him, examining the delicate jewelry now lying in the middle of his hand. A frown spread across his forehead as he stared at the pendant. It soon emitted a subtle glow, barely noticeable to mortal eyes.

"What the–?" he murmured as he lifted his hand to eye level.

Tilting his head to the side, Apollo watched as the glow grew stronger. Pulses of light radiated from the center of the ruby, branching out toward the edges of the gold heart. The light would then rush back to the center a second or so later. He lost sense of time as he watched the luminosity's trajectory, trying to make sense of what he was seeing. A slight gasp broke his concentration several minutes later as his mother materialized beside him on the bench.

"Where did you get that?" she asked, reaching out to try and take the pendant from him.

Apollo closed his fingers around the necklace and held it out of her reach. "I found it," he said, the hairs on the back of his neck standing on end.

Leto's eyes narrowed with suspicion. "How? Where?"

"Does it matter?"

Her lips pursed with displeasure. "Don't lie to me, Apollo. Where–?"

"I can't tell you, Mom. Let's leave it at that."

She sighed with dismay and shook her head. "Can I see it, at least?"

His fingers tightened around the delicate metal. "You'll give it back?"

"Of course."

He chewed on the lower right corner of his lip before he deposited the necklace into her waiting hands. Leto clutched the pendant with shaky fingers. She traced a fingertip along the heart's outer edge, watching as it began to glow once more. The pulsing light intrigued her, and she bent forward to examine the ruby.

"Do you know what this is?" she asked, her voice barely a whisper.

"No."

Leto straightened and pinned her dark brown eyes upon him. "It's a receptacle."

"A what?"

"A container, one that's infused with power."

Apollo snatched the necklace from her hand, and held it in front of his face between a thumb and forefinger. "How is that possible? It's just a necklace!"

"It's quite possible. Most especially when something or someone needs to be contained."

He stared at his mouth with bewilderment. "There's a person stuck inside this thing?"

"No," she said. "I don't think so."

"But . . . ?"

She rubbed an index finger across the bridge of her nose. "Think about it, Apollo. You're a god, for Pete's sake! No ordinary person can infuse an object. You should know that."

His eyes widened. "Only we can."

"Yes."

He glanced at the necklace. "So what's in here, then?"

"Power, and lots of it."

Apollo's eyes were drawn to the pendant once more. The light inside the jewel blinked repeatedly as he stared it. He saw, then, what he hadn't seen before–a whirlpool of purple and blue colors swirling in the ruby's center. His eyes closed of their own volition as he tried to sense the power contained within the jewel.

Try as he might, he couldn't pinpoint who it belonged to. Though he could now see the power held within the pendant, he couldn't breach the wards that surrounded it. Someone had taken extreme precautions when it came to the power the necklace contained.

Why would someone hide such a thing? Who does this power belong to? he wondered, knowing that he was holding an item of great significance. *How did my cousin come to have it within his possession? Does he even know what's inside this thing?*

"Talk to me," Leto said, drawing his attention once more. "What aren't you telling me?"

Apollo glanced at his mother out of the corner of his eye. He shook his head and transported the necklace back to its hiding place. Strengthening the wards he'd set around his vault, he leaned back against the bench, and ran an unsteady hand through his hair.

"I'm fucked," he said.

Leto reached out to curl hand around his left shoulder. "Darling—"

He brushed her hand aside and stood up. "I've got to go."

"Won't you at least tell me what's going on?"

"Not yet."

"When?"

"Soon, Mother. Soon. What are you doing here, anyway?"

"I came to talk to you. We left quite few things unsaid."

A rush of color flooded his cheeks. "I know, but . . ."

She sighed. "Your loyalty to your sister prevents you from saying a word."

"Yes."

Leto came to stand in front of him, and reached out to curl her hands around his flushed cheeks. She gently drew his head down to place a soft kiss upon his forehead.

"Be careful, my son," she said, and promptly teleported herself home.

CHAPTER 9

Medusa leaned against the doorjamb leading to her daughter's room, watching as her daughter rummaged through her jewelry box. Callidora's brow was furrowed with concentration, and she took no notice of her lounging nearby. The young woman flitted about the room, tossing various items aside with frustration.

"Is everything OK?" she asked, crossing her arms about her chest.

Callidora paused in the middle of what she was doing to glance at her mother. "No. My necklace is missing."

Medusa's blue eyes narrowed. "What necklace?"

"The one you gave me for my sixteenth birthday. I can't find it."

A ripple of apprehension coursed down Medusa's spine. She knew well of the necklace her daughter spoke of. The golden heart with a ruby embedded in its middle was a gift she'd bestowed upon her three years ago. It frightened her to know that it might have gone missing.

Her mind raced with the implications of what it could mean if the pendant turned up in the wrong hands.

She pushed herself away from the door and entered the room. "Do you remember where you left it?"

"No. Well, yes, but it's not here anymore."

"Where did you last leave it?"

Callidora pointed to the vanity. "Here. I think."

"You think, or you don't know?"

"I do! It was here. I swear it!"

The hairs on the back of Medusa's neck stood on end. "You've misplaced it, that's all."

"No! I remember where I left it, Mom!"

The sound of Callidora's rising voice drew Alexandros' attention. He soon appeared, frowning as he caught sight of Medusa's worried gaze.

"Is everything all right?" he asked.

"No. My necklace is missing."

"Honey–"

Callidora rolled her eyes at her mother. "Don't say it!"

Medusa sighed and shook her head. "Fine, then. I won't."

Alexandros' eyes narrowed. "What necklace?"

"The gold heart with the ruby in it."

His mouth thinned to a tight line. "It's probably around here somewhere."

"It's gone. Someone took it."

"You don't know that," Medusa said.

A muscle twitched along Callidora's lower jaw. "How else would it go missing?"

She shrugged. "You don't remember where you left it, obviously."

"But I do!" Callidora stamped her foot with impatience and pointed at her dresser. "It was right there!"

"Darling–" The look her daughter gave her cut off the rest of her reply.

"You know what? Get out!"

"Dora . . ."

"Get out!" Callidora cried as she pushed her mother and Alexandros back through the open door.

Her daughter's strength surprised her. It was a sign that the wards surrounding the necklace were weakening. Which meant that she'd soon come into her own powers. That, she knew, would not bode well. Callidora had no idea what her powers were like, much less how to use them. One wrong move, and chaos would erupt around her.

CHAPTER 10

Medusa hurried to her room with Alexandros at her heels. He slammed the door shut behind him, and moved forward to pull her to him. She sidestepped his advance and walked over to the panoramic window overlooking Central Park. Her hands shook as she grasped the windowsill, unable to curb the thoughts running rampant through her mind.

"Talk to me," Alexandros said.

"What is there to say?" she asked, allowing him to wrap his arms around her.

"You've reservations about the necklace."

"Of course, I do. It's gone, Alex. In the wrong hands . . ."

Alexandros' hold on her tightened as she melted against him. "Why would someone want to filch something so mundane?"

Horror clouded Medusa's eyes. "Mundane? Nothing about Callidora is mundane, much less that necklace. We bound her powers from the moment she was born. That pendant is her legacy. One we bequeathed her from an early age."

"A legacy that will be found."

She broke free of his embrace and stormed across the room to throw herself across the bed. "You don't know that!" she cried as she buried her face within her own pillow.

Alexandros approached the bed and sat down beside her. He flattened a hand against the small of her back, and moved his fingers about in a gentle soothing motion.

"There must be a plausible explanation for the missing necklace, Αγάπη. We'll find it soon. I'm sure of it."

Medusa rolled onto her back and stared up Alexandros with dismay. "What if we never find it, Alex? She'll be coming into her powers soon enough. Without that necklace, there's no way for her to channel the overflow."

"What if a similar necklace were to be created? We could then channel her powers into it."

Several tears leaked out of the corners of her eyes as she shook her head. "It won't work. I'm not a goddess."

"No, you're not, but you do have powers, Tasha. You're a Gorgon. A rare breed. You also have the powers Hades bestowed upon you when he changed your entire existence. I admit I don't like his having done so, but it was the only way to protect you from Athena's wrath. For that, I am grateful. With my help, we will find that necklace."

Medusa sat up and wiped her hands across her cheeks. "Can you summon it?"

"The necklace?"

"Yes. You helped infuse it so that we could channel Dora's powers into it. Surely, you can sense it?"

Alexandros clasped her hands in his and closed his eyes. He called forth an image of the necklace in his mind. Drawing it forward, he sent a burst of his power into the aether. A slight buzzing sound reverberated through his skull. His lips thinned to a tight line as he tried to pinpoint the direction from which the sound came from. Yet as soon as he connected with it, the buzzing disappeared. Something, or someone, was keeping the necklace heavily guarded, making it difficult for him to summon it to him.

"Nothing?" Medusa asked as he let go of her hands.

"I picked up a sense of it."

"But . . . ?"

"I lost it as quickly as I sensed it. My guess is someone is protecting it from outside influences."

"Is it possible that someone has discovered its true purpose?"

Alexandros shrugged and ran a hand through his raven curls. "It's hard to say."

Dread coursed through Medusa's body as she thought about the fact that someone had taken her daughter's necklace. *Has someone discovered my secret?* she wondered. *Do they know about who and what Callidora truly is?*

Sensing her distress, Alexandros pulled Medusa into his arms once more. He buried his face within the fragrant curls of her hair, hoping to offer her a little reassurance. She melted against him, burying her face against the curve of his shoulder. His mere presence soothed her, and she was grateful of the fact that she'd found him so long ago.

The *God of Wrath* wasn't easy to get along with, yet he seemed to mesh with her in ways she couldn't explain. Though volatile, he possessed a gentle nature that he didn't show to a good many. He'd done so much for her and her daughter, something none of the other gods or goddesses would have done. Granted, no one, aside from those privy to her precious secret, knew of her true existence. A secret, she knew, would be her ultimate undoing.

Though Alexandros protected that secret and more, his involvement with her went against everything Athena and the rest of the gods and goddesses had decreed so long ago. For all she knew, they'd try him for treason should the truth ever come to light. Still, he was her everything. More so than Hades had ever been. She'd die for him, and he knew it.

"It won't come to that," Alexandros said, moments later.

"Hmmm?"

"Your dying for me. It will never come to that."

"You read my thoughts again?"

He grinned as she pulled away from him. "It's hard not to. You broadcast them quite loudly to me."

A flush of color stained her cheeks. "I–I'm sorry."

"Don't be. I'm the only one that can hear them. I

masked your signatures from the rest of the pantheon. Well, aside from Hades."

"You don't like him."

"Not that much, no. But I can't begrudge him all that he's done for you. Without his efforts, you wouldn't be here right now. Nor would Callidora exist."

She sighed and blinked rapidly to combat the sudden rise of her tears. "I'm afraid, Alex. What if we–?"

He pressed a finger to her lips to silence her. "Don't think it. We'll find the necklace before it's too late."

"And if we don't?"

"May the gods have mercy on the fool for what they've inadvertently set into motion."

Medusa grimaced, fighting the pain that now roiled within her. "That's what I'm afraid of," she said, aware of the fact that there was no way to escape the inevitable.

CHAPTER 11

Apollo gathered his composure and whisked himself to Deivos' apartment once more. A soft giggle assailed his hearing as he walked into his cousin's living room. Sprawled across Deivos' love seat was his sister, Artemis. Deivos leaned over her, pressing kisses to her engorged breasts. Both were oblivious to his presence.

"Artemis!" he roared, his blood boiling at the sight.

Though Hermes and Dionysus had previously mentioned that his sister and cousin were consorting with one another, he hadn't wanted to believe it. He'd thought himself as the only man in Artemis' life. Now, he knew better.

Artemis' silvery-yellow eyes sprung open. She pushed against Deivos' shoulders and reached for her tunic, doing her best to cover her nakedness. Deivos turned to face Apollo, a smile of satisfaction darting across his lips.

"Cousin!" Deivos purred. "What brin's ya 'ere?"

Apollo crossed his arms about his chest, his blue eyes

narrowed. "I came to speak with you, but I see you're otherwise engaged."

Deivos stood and adjusted the crotch of his pants. His erection strained against the leather.

"Why, in the bloody blazes, do ya keep poppin' up announced?"

"I go where I please."

Artemis tugged her tunic into place and glared at her brother. "Must you always ruin everything?"

"Had I known you were here, I wouldn't have come. Then again, I would never have known about this . . . this . . . How can you consort with him!?"

She shrugged, a knowing smirk flitting across her lips. "You have your lovers, Apollo, and I have mine," Artemis said as she approached Deivos and scraped her nails across his bare chest.

Deivos flinched as she drew blood. He glanced down at the red beads slowly forming across his flesh and sighed. Artemis reached out to wipe the blood away, and shoved her finger into her mouth.

"Mmmmm! Delicious!"

Apollo shuddered with distaste. "Are you done?"

"Hardly. Why are you here, Apollo?"

Deivos pulled Artemis against him, raking his mouth across hers. "Send him home. Let us finish what we started."

She giggled and nipped at his lower lip with her teeth. "OK."

Anger boiled deep within Apollo as he saw Deivos take liberties with his sister that were once his. He curled his right hand into a tight fist and drew upon his powers, ready to send his cousin to Tartarus. The look Artemis gave him, however, soon wiped all thought from his mind. Desire ran rampant in her eyes. She might have been enjoying her earthly delights with his cousin, but her passion belonged to Apollo alone.

"What do you know of that necklace I took from you, Deivos?" he asked, diving into the heart of the matter to keep himself from doing something irrational.

Deivos let go of his sister and turned to face him. "Not much. Why?"

"Where did you get it?"

"I filched it from someone."

"Yes, but who?"

"A woman."

"Who?"

Artemis paled considerably and wrapped a trembling hand around Deivos' right bicep. "Deivos . . ."

His cousin growled and freed his arm from her tight grasp. "The woman in the copy o' 'at picture ya showed me. It's 'ers."

"I gathered as much. Why is she so important?"

"Don't tell him!" Artemis cried.

Deivos glanced at her out of the corner of his eye. "'E knows. Somewhat."

"So?"

"So if ya want thin's to go the way ya want 'em to, yer gonna 'ave to tell 'im."

She pouted and shook her head. "I don't want to. Not yet."

"If ya dun do it, I will."

"You wouldn't!"

Deivos nodded. "I will. I'm done wit' all this secrecy. 'E already knows some of this, Love. It's only fair."

Artemis blinked, refusing to let her tears fall. "No! I forbid it."

Apollo cried out as she tossed a ball of energy in his direction. It enveloped him, rendering him immobile. His sister approached him, her mouth thinned to a tight line.

"Forgive me, brother," she said as a wave of darkness claimed him.

CHAPTER 12

Apollo awoke to find himself chained to a cold stone wall. Silver handcuffs chafed the skin of his wrists as he tried to pull them free. Try as he might, they refused to break open. He tried to summon forth a burst of his power and failed. The room he now found himself in was heavily warded, preventing him from accessing what was rightfully his.

Closing his eyes, he searched deep within himself for the flame of power that slowly ebbed away by the second. He tried to hold onto it to no avail. Someone had made sure that the surrounding force field would heavily negate a person's powers. He strongly suspected that Artemis was behind the machinations of the room he now found himself in.

As if his very thought had summoned her, Artemis strode into the room with a knowing smirk on her face. Her fiery red hair was pulled into a loose chignon on top of her head, her silvery-yellow eyes snaking up and down his writhing body. She wore a white-colored peplos that loosely draped her womanly curves. Her nipples strained against the fabric as their gazes clashed.

Apollo felt his body react to the sight, aching to pull her tight against him. Artemis' eyes darkened as she stared back at him. Against his better judgment, his cock grew hard, straining against the dark jeans he wore. He wanted her, more so now than ever. Yet he knew she would deny him what he wanted the most.

"Comfy?" she asked as she walked up to him.

"You call this comfortable?" He tugged at the cuffed chain holding his right arm in place.

Artemis came to a stop before him. "You brought this upon yourself, brother."

"Did I?"

She nodded. "Yes."

"How?"

"You know how."

His eyes narrowed as he stared down at her. "I was only doing what you told me to."

"Were you?"

"Artemis!"

"You've been holding out on me, Apollo."

"No, I haven't."

Artemis reached out to scrape her nails across his jaw. "Haven't you?"

Apollo winced as she drew blood, though he refused to give her the satisfaction of letting her know just how much it hurt.

"I deserve answers, Artemis."

She smiled and drew his head down just enough so that she could brush her lips against his. "Yes, I know," she said, and took a step back to assess him once more.

"Stop playing games with me. Be honest, for once!"

Artemis laughed and twirled about in front of him. "Why? There's no fun in that."

"Artemis . . ."

She stopped dancing and turned to face him. A cold, calculating light invaded the depths of her eyes. Though he wasn't sure as to how or what it was, something has changed. Artemis no longer resembled the loving woman he'd once known. In her place stood a cold, callous, and calculating woman that was only out for herself. She'd shown him that fact many times ever since she'd come to him about the *Child of Calamity*, but he'd refused to see it. Now, he knew better.

"What do you want?" he asked, moments later.

"From you? Nothing."

"Bullshit!"

Artemis grinned and moved toward him once more. She pressed herself against him, cupping his aching cock. His body betrayed him, and he found himself pushing against the palm of her hand. A strangled moan escaped him as she squeezed the tip of his penis.

"You seem to be foiling my every plan, brother. I can't have that."

"Plan? What plan? You haven't even told me everything!"

"I've told you enough. The fact that you've gone snooping about makes things even harder to bear. You should have kept your mouth shut, Apollo!"

"I haven't–"

She swung the back her hand across his left cheek, the sound of the slap reverberating throughout the room. "Too many people know about the child now. You should have left well enough alone. I could have taken care of everything!"

Apollo glared at her and struggled against the chains that kept him bound to the stone wall. "I've no idea what you're talking about!"

"Don't you?" she asked, increasing the pressure upon his throbbing cock.

He cried out from the pain, yanking his hips backwards in the hopes that she'd release him. Artemis did no such thing. Instead, she worked his penis free of his jeans, and wrapped her fingers tightly around it. In one smooth motion, she mounted him, impaling herself upon Apollo with more force than she'd intended.

Apollo cried out from the pain, hating the fact that his body was quick to respond to her unexpected assault. Artemis didn't care about the fact that she was hurting him. She sought retribution against him for the supposed slights he'd committed against her. One way or another, she'd make him pay.

She'd found the one true way for him to do just that. Against his will, he lost himself to the emotions coursing through his body. What Artemis wanted, she got, much to his own chagrin.

CHAPTER 13

Hours passed before Apollo found himself alone within his cell. Artemis had taken her pound of flesh and then some from him. He now hung in an awkward position against the wall, his pants and underwear pooled around his ankles.

Apollo yanked at the cuffs wrapped around his wrists with frustration. He hated the fact that his sister had left him there to rot. That she'd taken what he wasn't ready to give her against his will sat ill with him. The handcuffs rubbed against his flesh, drawing blood with his every movement. Though he'd worked his hand through a good portion of the cuffs, his efforts were futile. His hands were too large and would not allow him the leeway he needed to free himself, once and for all.

The door to his cell opened unexpectedly. Dyina, his cousin and current paramour, strode into the room. With care, she closed the door behind her and made her way over to him. Without uttering a single word, she slipped a set of keys out from beneath the folds of her peplos and unlocked the handcuffs. He fell to the floor, his body trembling from exhaustion. Dyina knelt beside him and flicked several strands of his hair behind his right ear.

"We need to hurry," she said.

Apollo glanced at her out of the corner of his eye. "My powers don't work here."

She produced a small glass vial full of a swirling blue and silver-colored liquid and uncapped it. With a quick flick of her hand, she tipped his head back and poured the liquid down his throat. His powers flared to the surface as the modified ambrosia coursed through his veins. Wrapping his arms around her, Apollo closed his eyes and teleported them to the one place he knew Artemis wouldn't follow–the palace he'd secured on the sunken island of Atlantis.

He landed in the middle of the throne room, and gently placed Dyina back on her feet. She smiled up at him, her blue eyes shining with adoration. A frown spread across Apollo's forehead as he stared down at her. How had she found him?

"You're wondering as to how I knew about where you were," she said as he let go of her.

The soiled clothes Apollo wore disappeared in the blink of an eye, and were promptly replaced with fresh counterparts. His nakedness hadn't affected her as much as he'd thought it would. Then again, she'd seen him in his birthday suit not too long ago.

"How *did* you know where I was?" he asked as he moved toward the massive gold throne sitting against the wall in the northernmost part of the room.

Dyina wrung her hands together and nervously shifted from foot to foot. "Artemis showed up at Zeus' palace."

He dropped onto the chair and curled a leg around the left armrest. "What on earth were you doing there?"

"Mother requested my presence, so I went to see her. I was walking through the main hall when Artemis showed up."

"So?"

"She wasn't alone."

A bitter laugh burst from Apollo's lips. "When is she not alone?"

She stamped her feet with frustration. "You're not listening!"

"Get to the point then."

Dyina glared at him and sighed with dismay. "Deivos was there. They were arguing about the prophecy concerning the *Child of Calamity*."

The hairs on the back of Apollo's neck to stood on end. "Go on."

"I hid behind one of the statues and overheard every word."

"I gathered as much, Dyina, but it doesn't–"

"They want Zeus' throne, Apollo. Deivos knows who the child is, and he's helping your sister in the hopes of keeping her true identity hidden."

"That's impossible!"

"It's not," Dyina said. "I was there."

"Did they mention the child's name?"

"No."

"The child is female?"

Dyina nodded. "That much was confirmed, Apollo. Your sister has plans for the girl. Artemis hopes to overthrow Zeus soon enough. To do that, she said she needs whatever it is you're keeping hidden."

Though Apollo had known part of Artemis' plans, she'd never truly clued him in on what she wanted or needed. She'd given him just enough information to keep him wrapped around her finger. The fact that Deivos seemed to know exactly what his sister was up to angered him. It drove home the pain and heartache about what she'd done to him.

He now knew that he needed to keep the child out of Artemis' grasp. Granted, he wasn't quite sure as to whether the girl he'd come across was truly the *Child of Calamity*. Nevertheless, she deserved to be kept safe and out of Artemis' sordid machinations. Prophecy or not, the girl was an innocent. Her safety was his main concern now, and he would do everything possible to thwart his sister's plans.

Apollo sat up straight and fixed his steely blue gaze upon her. "What else did they speak about?"

"You. About the fact that Artemis was keeping you locked up in one of her own dungeons on Mount Olympus."

"I was on Mount Olympus?"

She nodded, her dark blonde hair falling across her brow. "Yes."

"But . . ."

"Artemis was able to get someone to ward the room you were in so that it negates a god or goddess's powers. It allows her to have her way with whatever person she brings there. She assumed that you'd be putty in her hands. That you'd no longer question her as to what she wants to do with the child. At least, that's what she told Deivos."

"I see."

"Deivos asked her as to whether she'd stowed away the special ambrosia he'd acquired for her that would restore a god's powers while in the room. She confirmed it before they headed for the main hall."

"I'm guessing you infiltrated her personal quarters to get it so that you could rescue me?"

Dyina smiled. "Yes. I'd do anything for you, Apollo. You know that."

It warmed him to know that she was willing to sacrifice herself for him, but he knew that her having done so put her in danger. Once Artemis discovered what she'd done, her wrath would know no bounds. His sister had made it clear that he'd never leave the cell she'd thrown him into. With the security she'd placed around the room, she'd never thought about the fact that there might have been someone out there willing to set him free.

Hell, that thought alone had never crossed his mind either. That he was now here, hidden on the island of Atlantis with the beautiful Dyina by his side, made him cognizant of the fact that his sister had changed the game considerably. Nothing and no one was safe. Artemis was hell-bent on getting what she wanted. Deivos, obviously her consort, was lending her the helping hand she needed to achieve her very goals.

If he was to succeed in knocking his sister down, he needed to know exactly what his cousin was doing for and with her. Doing so, however, was easier said than done. Deivos was committed to helping Artemis at all cost. He'd never tell him what he wanted to know.

Apollo refused to play by Artemis' rules. His livelihood and that of the entire pantheon, not to mention the world itself, was at stake. Artemis needed to be stopped, and the *Child of Calamity* was his only means of turning the tables in his favor.

He stood up and stared down at his beloved with a soft smile playing about his lips. "You need to go home now, Dyina."

Her loving smile disappeared as she stared up at him. "But . . ."

He approached her and reached out to curl his hands around her cheeks. "I appreciate what you've done for me. We will speak more of this soon, but there's something I must now do. Go home, and tell no one of what's transpired today."

Her eyes glittered with unshed tears. "Will I get to see you soon?"

"Yes," he said, and bent down to brush his lips across hers.

Dyina wrapped her arms around him, savoring the kiss for all it was worth. Her shoulders shook as she held on to him for as long as she was able. She pulled away from him, moments later. Without another word, she dematerialized, leaving him alone once more.

Apollo glanced about the room, his mind racing with the implications of what he was about to do. He had an advantage over his sister, one he hadn't thought of until now. The necklace he'd confiscated from Deivos' penthouse was still in his possession. Someone out there knew about the pendant's true origins. Though he wasn't sure as to where he needed to start, Apollo knew of one person who could tell him more about the wretched prophecy–Zeus' wife, Hera.

CHAPTER 14

"What in the seven Hells of Tartarus are *you* doing here?" Hera asked.

She burst to her feet as Apollo materialized in the middle of her personal quarters. He smirked with amusement as her handmaidens scattered in every direction.

"There are no such seven hells in Tartarus, my queen," he said.

Hera glared at him as she dismissed her attendants. "So you think. What do you want, Apollo?"

"I'd like to talk to you."

She stared at him with disdain written across her alabaster features. "What could I possibly want to talk to you about?"

He produced a copy of the photograph Artemis had shown him not too long ago, and shot it through the air at her. Hera deftly caught the glossy paper between her fingers and glanced down at it. Her baby blue-colored eyes narrowed with suspicion.

"Where did you get this?" she asked as she crumpled the photograph into a tight ball.

"Never you mind. I've questions that need answering."

"What does this have to do with me?"

"Everything. Is she the *Child of Calamity*?"

The queen shrugged and tossed the ball of paper in Apollo's direction. He sidestepped the trajectory and shook his head at her.

"Perhaps," she said, and made her way back to the chaise lounge she'd been reclining on before he'd come upon her.

"I need to know, Hera."

She settled herself on the lounge and looked up at him once more. "What's it to you?"

A muscle twitched across Apollo's lower jaw. "I have no time for games, my queen. The safety and continuation of our beloved pantheon is at stake. I need to know everything you know about the *Child of Calamity*."

Hera's mouth thinned to a tight line. "What makes you think I'll tell you exactly what you want to know? I have no allegiance to you, your sister, or that wretched mother of yours."

"I haven't come here on their behalf. Nor have I forgotten what you did to me not to long ago, Hera. Unfortunately, I need answers, and you're the only one that can give them to me."

Hera regarded him through veiled eyes. Minutes passed. The silence between them thickened as she refused to say a word. Impatience rippled through every inch of Apollo's body as he waited. He wouldn't leave her quarters until she told him everything.

"How did you come to know about the child?" Hera asked.

"My sister."

"She told you?"

"Somewhat."

A plush chair materialized in thin air, slowly drifting to the floor.

Hera pointed to it and said, "Have a seat."

"I don't—"

The look she gave him cut off his reply. Apollo took a seat, wiping his damp palms across the tattered knees of his jeans.

"Artemis knows of the child, then?"

"Yes."

"Who told her about it?"

Apollo shrugged. "We all know of the prophecy, Hera."

Her lips pursed with concentration. "You all know what Zeus and I want you to know. That doesn't mean you know everything there is to know about it."

He crossed his arms about his chest. "Enlighten me, then."

"I don't think you're ready for that kind of enlightenment," she said, her head tilted slightly to the side.

He growled with frustration, hating himself for what he was about to say. "My *sister* is hell-bent on knocking my father down a peg or two, you witch. If I'm going to stop her from achieving her goals, I'm going to need you to be honest with me."

Hera snorted with derision. "How is my help going to help you do just that? Many have tried to take my husband's throne, Apollo. They have failed. Artemis will be no different."

"Artemis is slowly amassing the means to take him down," he said as beads of perspiration broke out across his forehead.

"How?" she asked, remaining calm and collected. "There's nothing she can do to change the way things are."

"The prophecy is the key, Hera. You know it, I know it, and so does Zeus."

Hera's face paled beneath the onslaught of his words. "How do you know so much?"

"I know only what my sister has made me privy to. The rest I've made assumptions on all my own."

"There's no way—"

"Who and where is the child?"

"I don't know," she said a tad too quickly.

"You're lying."

"I'm not!"

"Surely, you must have some sort inkling!?"

"Well, yes, but—"

Apollo jumped to his feet and stared down his nose at her. "Help me, Hera. Artemis must be stopped!"

She gazed up at him with uncertainty shining in the depths of her eyes. He was well aware of the fact that she was reluctant to help him. Who wouldn't be? His father was the king of all the gods. The power Zeus possessed had gotten him to where he was now. If he so chose, his father could enslave them all. Hera knew that just as much as he did.

"If I help you . . ."

"Yes?"

"It will come with a price."

Apollo nodded. "I gathered as much."

"We must start from the beginning."

"All right."

"Are you sure of this?"

"Yes."

"There will be no going back once your eyes have been opened."

"I know that."

She stood up and held out a hand to him. "Take my hand."

Apollo clasped her hand without question. A bright light erupted between them. Hera stared up at him as the glow grew stronger. Warmth crept across every inch of his body as Hera drew closer to him. She smiled as she wrapped her arms around his waist. Hugging her to him, he closed his eyes, allowing her to take him on a ride that would forever change his life from that moment on.

CHAPTER 15

"Where are we?" Apollo asked as the light surrounding them dissipated.

"Hush," Hera said as she pointed to something in the distance. "Pay attention."

Apollo watched as his surroundings solidified. Beneath a Syrian Juniper tree sat a younger-looking Hera. Her auburn tresses fluttered in the breeze. A soft smile played about her lips as she gazed into the distance, her hands curled demurely across her lap.

Though he wasn't sure as to why Hera had brought him back to this moment in time, he knew it served a purpose. He'd asked for her help in bringing his sister down. What he would do soon enough would act as a grand betrayal against Artemis. He wasn't going to let her get away with ruining his life and that of the entire pantheon. If what he was about to witness would give him the needed leverage to stop his sister, once and for all, he'd gladly take it and more.

235

The younger version of Hera sighed and produced a tightly rolled scroll from thin air. She unrolled it as a small table materialized before her and floated to the ground. Several quick flicks of her hands manifested an inkwell and a long writing quill. Hera uttered a quick spell and flattened the parchment against her makeshift desk.

"What is she—*you*—writing?" Apollo asked as he stood beside the *Queen of the Gods*.

Hera smiled and turned to face him. "Don't you know?"

He shook his head, several errant curls falling across his brow. "No."

The queen spread her arms wide, her smile lengthening by the second. "This, my dear boy, is where it all began. I concocted a plan that would keep my husband's beloved pantheon under lock and key. In this very garden is where I crafted the prophecy that would forever change the world as we knew it."

"Why?"

Hera's smile faltered. "Why not?"

"Do you have any idea what you've done?"

"What I've done? I saved our way of life, Apollo. Zeus needed a means to keep everyone and everything in line. The prophecy ensured that would happen."

Apollo glanced at the ghost of Hera's past as she penned her deadly missive. The prophecy had wreaked havoc on his life ever since it had been brought to his attention. It fueled Artemis' desires and made her do things she normally didn't do.

If only Hera hadn't changed the way things were before, he thought. Apollo hated the fact that his life and those of his brethren had been changed in such a drastic manner.

"You can change it, can't you?"

Hera's eyes narrowed with suspicion. "Change what?"

"The past. Surely, you can undo the prophecy?"

"Why would I do that?"

"That wretched prophecy is what's driven my sister to seek retribution against our father. If Zeus goes down, so do we."

"Nonsense!" Hera said. "Zeus will never relinquish what's his. Not even for your sister."

"Don't you get it!?" Apollo cried. "She's going to find a way to make that golden throne hers."

Hera laughed and tossed her auburn curls over her left shoulder. "How? She's just one of the many insignificant gods that contribute nothing to our way of life. Nothing she could do will change the way things are."

Apollo stared down at her, a muscle flinching across his jaw. He knew well that Hera's claims of Artemis' not being a threat weren't true. He'd seen what she could do. It was only a matter of time until she disrupted life as they knew it. Everyone, both mortal and immortal, would suffer because of it.

Hera dismissed his claims because she felt that she'd be able to control his sister when the time came. He knew well that she wouldn't be able to. If Artemis succeeded in gaining the child's allegiance, she'd destroy the little that was left of the world around her.

Against his better judgment, Apollo cleared his throat and said, "Artemis is close to finding the *Child of Calamity*, Hera."

CHAPTER 16

The dream world collapsed around them as Apollo's words took Hera by surprise. She glared at him, her mouth pursed with displeasure. His softly spoken words had thrown her for a loop. Hera was no longer sure as to whether the ball was still in her court.

"There's no way such a thing is possible."

"Why not?"

Hera flicked a hand at him with avid dismissal. "The child doesn't exist."

Apollo frowned. "It doesn't?"

"No."

"But—"

The look she gave him cut off the rest of his reply.

"The prophecy is a lie," she said, hating the fact that she'd told him the truth.

Apollo's eyes narrowed as he turned to face her. "No, it isn't."

Hera shook her head at him with vehemence. "It is. I

invented it."

"So you invented it. Big deal! The fact remains that the child exists."

"You believe it does, but it does not. If such were the case, Zeus and I would know it."

"If you didn't believe in the child's existence, you wouldn't have had your cronies beat me up over it."

She shrugged. "That was a minor technicality. The goal was to find out how much you knew about the prophecy itself."

"I gathered that much, Hera. You understand, then, that sometimes a lie can become truth."

"I've said no such thing."

"Not openly, no."

Hera stamped her foot with impatience. "Stop psycho-analyzing me!"

Apollo strode toward the chaise lounge she'd occupied not too long ago and sat down. "Sorry!"

His intense scrutiny unsettled her. Hera became aware of the fact that Apollo wasn't as forthcoming about everything as she thought he'd be. Her stepson was holding quite a bit back, though she wasn't sure as to why.

She assumed it was because his loyalties to Leto and his sister kept him from divulging everything. Granted, he'd said enough. It lay to rest her reservations about what Artemis was up to. The girl wanted her husband's throne, and would do everything possible to claim it. That she'd utilize the prophecy to do so spoke volumes.

Artemis believed in the child's existence. Whether

she'd found someone who fit the bill was hard to say, but she had a feeling that the goddess would produce such a being when the time came. It wouldn't matter if the child was mortal or demigod. As long as he or she fulfilled the prophecy, that was all that mattered.

"I'm going to need a bit of time to come up with a suitable plan to thwart your sister's advances."

"We don't have time."

"Make it. We cannot allow Artemis to spring this supposed child on us all."

"What do you want me to do?"

"Keep an eye on your sister, and report everything she does to me."

"And if I fail?"

Hera smiled, a cold, calculating light invading the depths of her eyes. "I'll throw you into deepest, darkest reaches of Tartarus, where no one will ever know you still live."

Apollo's mouth thinned to a tight line. He nodded and dematerialized, leaving her alone once more.

Hera stared at the spot he'd occupied with perplexion. She no longer doubted that things were changing inside the pantheon itself. Artemis was hell-bent on destroying everything as they knew it, something she would not allow. If achieving peace meant that she'd have to kill the goddess in the process, she'd do it. There was no way she was going to lose what rightfully belonged to her.

CHAPTER 17

Callidora sat down on the edge of her bed and sighed with dismay. Her favorite necklace was still missing. She remembered leaving it on top of her chest of drawers several days ago. In her mind, that was the safest place for it. Yet it wasn't there. Her parents were convinced that she'd misplaced it, but she knew better. Someone had clearly taken it, though she had no idea as to whom.

Why would anyone want such a thing? she wondered. *It's just silly old thing!*

She sighed and pushed herself to her feet. Walking out onto the adjoining balcony, Callidora stared at the Manhattan skyline. The sky was full of vivid indigos, oranges, dark blues, and pink colors. It was a sight she never grew tired of. Today, however, it brought her no joy to experience such splendor.

Her mind was preoccupied with the theft of her necklace. It mind-boggled her that someone could stoop so low. That someone purposefully invaded her privacy scared her beyond belief. A slight shiver coursed down her spine as question after question tumbled through her mind. She wrapped her arms around herself, and casually leaned against the railing.

How had she garnered such attention from someone? Was it something she'd done without knowing? Would she be able to deflect this person's attentions in the long run?

"A penny for your thoughts," Hades said as he materialized beside her.

Callidora gasped with surprise and turned to face him. "How do you do that!?"

An innocent look crossed his face. "Do what?""

"Pop up when I seem to need someone the most."

Hades grinned. "Call it intuition. How are you, αγαπημένο παιδί μου?"

Another sigh slid past Callidora's lips. "I . . . It's been ages since you've called me your dearest child."

He reached out to curl his hands around her cheeks, and pressed a soft kiss to her forehead. "That's because you are that for me. I love you as if you were my own."

"You do?" she breathed as tears clouded her vision.

"Of course." He clasped her hands in his, and led her back into her bedroom. Taking a seat on the edge of her bed, he said, "What's wrong?"

She wiped her nose across the back of her hand, another wave of tears rising to the surface. "Nothing."

"Dora . . ."

Her shoulders slumped with defeat. "My favorite necklace is missing."

The hairs on the back of Hades' neck rose with apprehension. "What necklace?"

"The one Mom gave me. A golden heart with the ruby in the middle."

Hades' mouth thinned to a tight line. "Where did you leave it?"

"On the dresser."

"You probably misplaced it, that's all."

"Mom said the same thing, but I know I didn't. Someone took it."

"It's just a necklace, Dora."

Her head swung up with an audible pop. "Is it?" she asked, her voice barely a whisper.

Hades stared into her eyes. "Yes. I can get you another one."

Callidora shook her head at him. "I don't want another one."

"Then what do you propose I do?"

A light of determination shone in the depths of her cornflower blue eyes. "Find it," she said.

"How?"

"You're a god, aren't you?"

He pushed himself to his feet and walked toward the balcony once more. His shoulders were taut with tension as he stared at the darkening horizon.

"I am, but that doesn't mean I'll continuously abuse my given powers," he replied as he turned around to face her once more.

"How would searching for a necklace make that possible?"

Hades curled his hands into tight fists. "Dora . . ."

She jumped to her feet and ran in his direction, launching herself into his arms. "Please, Uncle!"

Hugging her close, Hades closed his eyes and buried his face within his daughter's citrus-smelling curls. "Of course, Αγάπη. I'll help."

"You will?" Callidora asked, pulling herself back to stare into his dark and troubled eyes.

"Yes, I'll help you."

Callidora smiled with appreciation and wrapped her arms around his waist once more. She took no notice of the waves of anger emanating from Hades himself. Instead, she focused on the fact that he was willing to help her get her necklace back somehow. That was all that mattered.

CHAPTER 18

Apollo returned to his home on Mount Olympus, his brow furrowed with consternation. He'd betrayed Artemis' trust in the hopes of stopping her from causing further harm. Hera promised that she'd come up with a plan to thwart his sister's advances, though he wasn't sure how helpful she'd be in the long run. Deep inside, he knew the queen could not be trusted. Not completely, anyway, but he had no other option available to him. For the time being, he needed Hera to believe that they were on the same side.

His body clamored for rest. Ever since he'd learned about the prophecy, he'd ignored most of his duties. Though the sun rose and fell when it was supposed to, he didn't pay much attention to the world around him. That, he knew, had to change. If he was going to stop Artemis' underhanded shenanigans, he needed to be at the top of his game.

Striding into his bedroom, Apollo stopped within his

tracks. His eyes widened as he stared at Artemis as she lay naked upon his bed. She turned to face him, a knowing smile darting across her lips.

"You're finally home," she said as she stretched out before him.

His mouth grew dry as he took in the sight of her flesh on display. "W–What are you doing here?"

She feigned a pout, curling a loose strand of her fiery mane around one of her fingers. "Am I not welcome here?"

"Yes, of course, but–"

Artemis sat up, her breasts heaving with every breath she took. "But?"

Apollo composed himself and closed the door behind him as he took another step into the room. "I thought you'd be lying in Deivos' bed right about now."

A slight grimace spread across Artemis' face. "I–No, not really. I've better things to do than spend an entire day in his bed."

He quirked a brow at her in question. "Such as?"

His sister swung her legs over the side of the bed and pushed herself to her feet. Her smile broadened as her gaze clashed with Apollo's. The sight of her delectable body wreaked havoc on his libido. Though he wanted nothing more than to sink into her warm folds, he knew he could not. Artemis was a distraction he could do without.

"We need to talk," she said as she walked in his direction.

Apollo made a beeline for the pitcher of wine lying

on the table. He poured himself a glass and gulped it down in one drink. The carafe vanished before he could pour himself another. He turned around to find Artemis fully clothed in front of him.

"Don't you want to play?" she asked, sounding a little coy.

"Not right now, no."

"Why not?"

"I'm tired, Artemis. Can we do this later?"

She frowned and shook her head at him. "We're doing this now."

He sighed with exasperation and dropped onto the nearest chair. "Fine! What is it now?"

Artemis smirked at him and sat down upon his lap. Apollo stiffened. He grabbed the chair's armrests, praying that he'd be able to resist both his body's urges and his sister's charms. She grinned at him, aware of how much she affected him.

"I've been patient, Apollo."

"Have you?"

She nodded. "Yes."

"But?"

"I'm done waiting."

"For?"

Her eyes narrowed as she stared down at him. "For everything. You, the child, and the whole stinking pantheon!"

"Artemis—"

She held up a hand to silence him. "Don't. Nothing you can say or do will change my mind, brother. It's time to act. Time to find out if my suspicions about the child are indeed true."

"Your suspicions, Sister, are nothing more than assumptions."

"No, they're not," she retorted. "The child exists, Apollo. Deny it all you want, but the end of our father's reign is near."

Apollo shot to his feet, tossing his sister to the floor. "Father is many things, Artemis, but he's still our father," he said, and marched toward the panoramic window. "He's had our best interests at heart."

Artemis cried out with surprise and glared at him as she pulled herself to her feet. "Our best interests at heart? Oh, please! Everything Daddy dearest does is for his benefit, not ours."

"He tries his best. You've got to give him credit for that."

She snorted with derision. "I don't have to give him credit for anything. I suppose you've taken his side, then?"

He turned around to face her. "What? No! It's just . . ."

"Just what? I thought you were on my side!"

"I am, but . . . There's far too much at stake."

"Too much at stake? Please. The *Child of Calamity* is our ticket to making Mount Olympus a better place. Don't you want more freedom? To live life however you see fit?"

"I do, but not at the cost of losing everything I hold dear. The child's existence hinders our own, Artemis."

"Nonsense!" she cried, her silvery-yellow eyes dark with fury. "He or she is our sole means of changing everything!"

"Father's presence on the throne keeps the Titan's at bay. Remove him, and they'll come back with a vengeance. Not even the presence of the child can detain them."

Artemis laughed and rolled her eyes. "Is that what worries you?"

"No, but—"

"The child is the *Harbinger of Chaos and the Destroyer of Worlds.* With his or her help, we can defeat the Titans should they rise again."

His lips thinned to a tight line. "You don't get it. The prophecy speaks of destruction. Lives will be lost. God or mortal, it won't matter. Is that what you want for us?"

Artemis' features blanched as she stared at him with disbelief. A muscle twitched along her lower jaw as she tried to rein in her wayward emotions. Soon, a loud pop reverberated throughout his quarters as she orbed herself away.

Apollo sighed and shook his head with dismay. He hated the fact that he'd caused her such displeasure, but he'd only told her the truth. Whether she wanted to admit it or not, the *Child of Calamity* would be their undoing. She'd set events into motion that would have dire consequences. Events, he surmised, that would wipe out life as they knew it. As much as it pained him, he knew he had to stop Artemis' plans, no matter the cost. In time, she'd thank him for taking matters into his own hands.

EPILOGUE

A sigh of relief escaped him as he spun the safe's dial to the left. The sharp click was music to his ears. Tugging the heavy door open, he eyed the various treasures stowed within.

His hands itched with the urge to take whatever he saw fit, but he knew he couldn't do so. He'd come to fetch the one item that had taken Artemis' fancy. Should he take more than he was supposed to, the theft would be noticed.

No, he thought. *Better to play it safe.*

He eyed the golden heart with a ruby embedded in its middle. From the moment he'd laid eyes on it, it had drawn him in like a moth to a flame. The pendant oozed with power, though he couldn't figure out as to who had imbued it to begin with. That it belonged to his current prey made the necklace more appealing.

Reaching out to clasp the pendant in his hand, he drew it toward him, running the tip of his right index finger across its smooth surface. He smiled and pocketed it, swinging the safe's door closed once more. In the blink of an eye, he was gone, leaving no trace of his presence within the room behind.

Coming in 2016.

The first book in *The Child Of Calamity* prequel series.

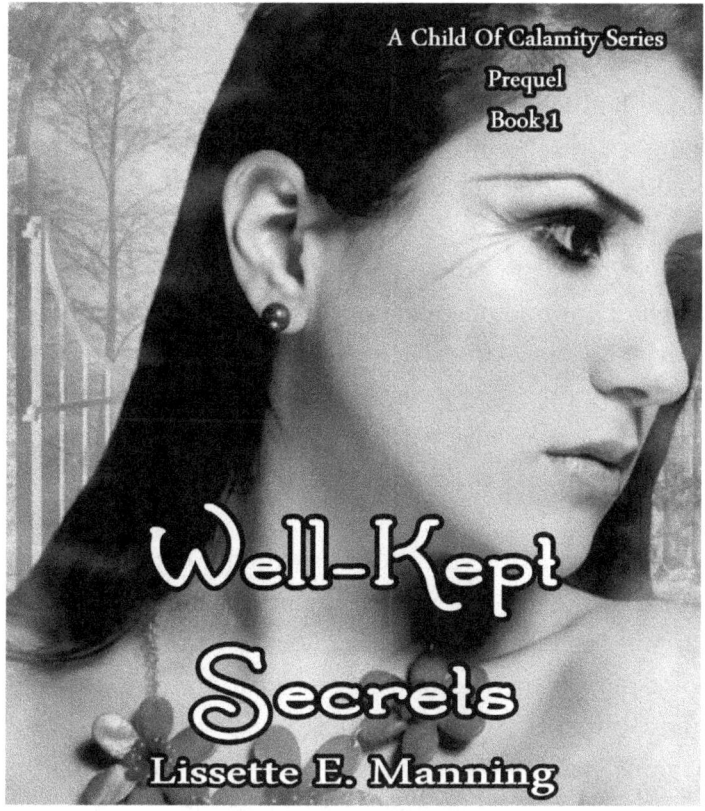

A Child Of Calamity Series
Prequel
Book 1

Well-Kept

Secrets

Lissette E. Manning

Please Note: This is not the book's actual cover.

The truth is sometimes hard to bear.

From the moment news of *The Child Of Calamity* arrived on her doorstep, Leto knew things would never stay the same. Never once did she imagine that her precious daughter would use Zeus' sacred prophecy to achieve an end to her own means. Deep inside, she's always believed that goodness lay in Artemis' heart. That her daughter would use her powers for the better.

Leto knows that nothing good will come out of her daughter's sordid machinations. Though she doesn't quite understand what drives her, she knows she cannot allow Artemis to do as she pleases. Order must be maintained. She cannot risk Zeus' wrath yet again should her daughter continue on the path she currently treads.

Delving deeper into the secrets surrounding the prophecy, Leto is determined in understanding why Artemis is so hell-bent on changing life as they know it. Someone out there knows exactly what's going on. Somehow, some way, she's going to try to put a stop to Artemis' plans. To do that, however, she'll have to go back to the beginning, much to Zeus' chagrin.

ABOUT THE AUTHOR

Lissette E. Manning is an author from Connecticut. She has been writing since she was six-years-old, and enjoys giving life to the stories always brewing in her head. She enjoys reading, music, playing video games, spending time with friends and family, and is also a bit of a computer geek.

Connect With Her Online:

Email: lizziebeth1095@sbcglobal.net
Facebook: http://www.facebook.com/LissetteElizabethManning
Twitter: http://www.twitter.com/xLizzieBethx
Website: http://www.simplistik.org
Blog: http://www.simplistik.org/lissetteemanning
PInterest: http://pinterest.com/gethsemane95
Goodreads:
http://www.goodreads.com/author/show/4867044.Lissette_E_Man ning